DOÑA QUIXOTE

GOLD OF OPHIR

Leena Krohn

Doña Quixote and other citizens

◇

Gold of Ophir

Translated from the Finnish by Hildi Hawkins

CARCANET

First published in Great Britain in 1995 by
Carcanet Press Limited
402-406 Corn Exchange Buildings
Manchester M4 3BY

I should like to thank Soila Lehtonen for her help
in reading the translation in draft. – H.H.

Translated from the Finnish *Doña Quijote ja muita kaupunkilaisia*
Werner Söderström, Helsinki, copyright © 1983 Leena Krohn
and *Oofirin kultaa*, Werder Söderström, Helsinki, copyright © 1987 Leena Krohn

A CIP catalogue record for this book
is available from the British Library.
ISBN 1 85754 145 6

The publisher acknowledges financial assistance
from the Arts Council of England.

Set in 11pt Meridien by Bryan Williamson, Frome
Printed and bound in England by SRP Ltd, Exeter

Funded by
THE
ARTS
COUNCIL
OF ENGLAND

Contents

Doña Quixote and other citizens

Gold of Ophir

Serpula lacrymans

The secret of famine-bread

Home-sickness

The glow of the Gold-Washers

Left and right

Colour or ash

Doña Quixote and other citizens

Portraits

Do not make images. Everything exists.

Mirkka Rekola

The sparrow

I cannot forget that, on the cliffs in the park, I stepped on a wounded bird. Its helpless movement under my heel, its absolute softness.

When I raised my foot, it was still able to flutter on to a stone beneath a lime-tree. We watched it and, in front of us on the granite, it buried its beak in its feathers, and there was no more movement.

'A small sparrow and a great peace,' Doña Quixote said.

It was the first day of autumn; the weather had changed. Behind the lime-trees the blue perspective of the clouds darkened.

'In the winter we shall be able to ski to those islands, unless I am that sparrow,' she said.

Why did she say that? I felt, again, the suffering under my heel, as if it had been a human face.

Later, when we were walking on the beach, a choir was singing unceasingly: very clear, high voices, women's or boys'. It was an aria no one had heard before, and it was born in the masts and rigging of the yacht-club's boats.

When the sky blackens, I, too, become sombre.

'What is it?' asks Doña Quixote.

'I can't bear it,' I say. 'No, I really can't.'

'What is it you have to bear, then?' she asks, and I answer: 'To live here on this rubbish-heap of a star for another thirty or forty or fifty years.'

'You deserve a beating,' says Doña Quixote. 'They're not years at all.'

'Aren't they?' I'm amazed.

'No,' says Doña Quixote, 'they're days.'

I calculate that forty years make seventeen thousand six hundred sunsets.

'When you have seen them all,' says Doña Quixote, 'are you sure you won't want to see another one, and then another...'

six /

The darkness of mirrors

The city is full of dark rooms. One of them was in the fun fair. In fact, it was the whole of a small house.

From the outside, it was very unassuming: just a cabin painted in candy colours, meant for use only in summer. The inside walls and the roof were entirely covered in mirror glass; even the pillars that supported the roof were covered in mirrored casings.

The house was a kind of labyrinth: the entrance and exit had their own corridors, long and winding.

The house's name was the House of Laughter.

We took the children to the House of Laughter. We went in without paying, since the booth where tickets were sold was empty.

I laughed seldom, and constrainedly – did little more, really, than sneer. An ordinary mirror image is, for me, at least as strange as the reflections caused by the convex and concave mirror surfaces here.

I did recognise myself in the form of bottle and a pumpkin, with a barrel-like pancake-face and as tall as a flag-post. I recognised myself from the fact that the eyes of all these ghosts were inhabited by the same absence as my own. It made them even more ridiculous, but at the same time it felt bitter.

I thought that if I were to spend longer with my reflections, I would become confused with them, and no one would be able to say any longer where they had their origin.

But the children had fun. They ran around the House of Laughter and wanted me to admire their caricatures, their grins and their echoes.

Until the doors banged. It was an unmistakable noise, even behind the laughter: someone was slamming the doors and bolting them. Immediately afterwards, the lights went out. Darkness slipped out from behind the mirrors, over the mirrors, down to the bottom of the mirrors. As if it had been there all the time, simply awaiting its opportunity.

For a moment, too, all sounds were absent, until I heard the children cry out.

'I'm here! I'm here!' I heard myself shout, and began to grope about me.

Strange: I really did exist, although the reflections had gone.

Their unseen arms wound themselves around my hips, and I told them all was well. We just had to wait.

We waited. The darkness had taken all the images. It had separated forms and reflections and put what only seemed to exist into its large pocket. But the darkness itself had countless reflections.

We waited. Nowhere is the darkness so deep as in the House of Laughter. From mirror to mirror it repeats itself and deepens, rises in a scream from the mirror's well only to fall into another chasm. Its echo is stronger than the scream itself.

We waited. And I was still not sure the reflections had really gone. Hidden by the darkness, they were waiting with us, as grotesque and unjust as before.

'If the minotaur exists,' I thought, 'it must live here, and all its swaying heads are our own.'

Someone flicked on a cigarette lighter. A little old man had joined us.

'This way,' he said, and set off in front of us. The flame wavered on the walls and the roof and all the reflections followed him, bottles and pumpkins, barrels and flag-poles.

When we got out of the House of Laughter, the sky was pale green as glass, but the coloured lights of the fun fair were already being switched on, all at once.

I had forgotten there were so many colours.

Straw

The winter had been hard, and a haze of indifference had surrounded me for a long time. My tongue was covered with a kind of film, and everything in life had lost its flavour. When I tried to grasp something, my hand became paralysed. A sticky substance isolated me from the world.

Early that spring, I met Doña Quixote for the first time. Where on earth was it? There, on the high hill where one can see the city and the harbour and the sea.

I was sitting on the pedestal of a statue when something passed me by. It was as long and thin as a piece of straw, and it moved so lightly that it seemed to slip along above the dust of the road. It had a pair of binoculars at its neck and it stopped by the railing and began to look out to sea.

The ice had just melted and the sea was breaking up into the year's first white horses. The piece of straw stood on the spot for so long and was so motionless that I soon forgot there was anyone there.

I, too, believed myself to be invisible. My coat was the same colour as the stone of the statue, and I imagined I blended unnoticeably into the fluttering clothes and noiseless cries of the cluster of people.

But the piece of straw had turned, and was examining the sculpture.

'What do you think?' she said.

'Are you speaking to me?' I said, alarmed.

'I can't see anyone else here,' she said calmly. 'Do you think they will be saved?'

'The shipwrecked people, you mean? I've never asked myself that. A statue isn't a story, you know,' I said smartly.

'No, that's true,' she conceded. 'But that cry – I've heard it elsewhere in this city. And then you start questioning... yourself, above all.'

'Do you get any answers?' I asked.

'I seldom answer,' she said. 'But I don't need to: life answers. It is generally a long and thorough answer.'

I looked at her more closely. Her face was like that of a mountain-dweller: lean, clear and fearless. Her eyes gazed out from among shadows, darkly brilliant and precise. She was dressed ascetically, in the Chinese mode: in a dark, military jacket and trousers.

'Is that what you do?' I asked, already a little interested. 'Ask yourself all kinds of questions?'

'Yes,' she conceded, looking at me distantly.

'And life answers?' I continued, a drop of derision spilling into my voice.

She eyed me now so penetratingly that I would have thought her gaze impudent had it not been unflinchingly tranquil.

She looked straight into my non-existence, at the spot where there is something like a needle-prick, but so deep that one could throw all one's belongings into it, one's memory and one's doubts, one's demands and one's subterfuges – yes, all one's life – and there would still be nothing at all there.

'I had a question in which I lived for a long time,' she said. 'Many years. And one day I remembered I had forgotten it. It had gone, and from that I knew that I had received an answer.'

Her words and her way of speaking baffled me. I turned to look at The Shipwrecked.

'I think they drown.'

'Perhaps you are right. They drown if no one hears them.'

Then she went on, looking at the sea, 'Once I wanted to be, for people, something like – like a piece of straw.'

It almost amused me. That was, after all, what she quite clearly was.

'Do you come here often?' I asked.

'Every Tuesday and Thursday.'

'Always?'

'Always,' she repeated, and tapped her binoculars. 'I have to be able to see the horizon.'

Then she turned. Without saying goodbye, and without paying any more attention to me, she began to descend the hill among the great lime-trees. Some of the trees were so old that they had great rents and hollow wounds, filled with asphalt and strengthened with iron bolts. Before I realised it, I was walking with her past The Wader, around whose thighs the water rippled, cold and indifferent.

At the steps that lead down to the street she stopped, took off a shoe and shook a couple of grains of sand from it. Shoe in hand, standing on one leg, she paused to think about something, like a large, old crane.

I was standing smiling a couple of steps above her when she raised her eyes. 'Oh, you're still there.'

She put her shoe back on.

'And I am here.'

She tapped on the step with her shoe. 'And where someone is standing, no one else can stand.'

That sentence – a self-evident truth, obviously enough, but above all the conviction with which she spoke it – touched my heart, which had long been silent and cold. She had begun to go down the steps again, but I did not follow her.

'Go wherever you like,' I said to her back. 'As far and for as long as you like. But there will come a Tuesday or a Thursday, fine or chilly...'

I had remained standing, my hand on the rail, and I saw, far away in the street, her hurrying, thin form. I looked at my own shoes and saw beneath them the granite step, the rose-pinkish stone and the glittering crystals, more living, more real, than many long years.

The place where you stand

And was it not stone, the very first thing I saw in this city?

It was everywhere, carved and uncarved, rough and polished until it shone. It was used to cover the surfaces of the squares and edge the narrow pavements. It formed the foundations of buildings; it was used to build steps and pedestals of statues and grandiose memorials to great men.

It pushed itself through subsoil and thin humus, like a forehead thinking a sombre thought, in parks, back yards and unbuilt sites. Even the roads that led to the city were cut and blasted through the same basic material. It was this place's plinth and raw material, it was the city's seal and destiny, like the sand of Rotterdam, the mud of Venice or the oil-shale of Pittsburgh...

I have seen a quiet street here, and a main road that is as busy as the river of Tuonela.[1] In a dream, I grew cabbages by its side, and the unbroken caravans of cars destroyed every single round head.

On the corner, under a large clock, is a coffee bar where one can buy grass and bootleg alcohol. One night there was an important meeting there, and I sat in the corner eating soup.

One of the participants in the meeting, a young man whom I half-knew, came up to me.

'May I?' he asked, and took the spoon from my hand. He fished something out of my plate of broth and, carrying the spoon held out in front of him, took it to show his own table.

'Look!' said the young man.

A murmur of disbelief and disdain filled the entire room. I tried to stretch my neck to see what was in the spoon, but

[1] The underworld in Finno-Ugrian mythology.

the young man held it up so high that I could not see anything.

From there I have walked here, to the quiet street. Here is the yard I have seen in a picture: a small back yard and a street musician, a small man with his violin. The walls were full of windows, but not one of them opened. Along the bottom of the picture was written, in a feeble hand, 'Alone with God'.

'To live under the eyes of others.' Open and closed, free and flowing spaces. Streets, rooms and yards. Staircases, squares and towers. Temples. Market-places. Bridges and steps, white ships. Faces that drift along the street like detached petals.

When the street-lights go on, the stone is no longer heavy. A deep glow lights up the patina of brick and plaster. The trees in the park are the evening's silhouette.

'Take note of the grace and softness that one can see, as one walks the streets, in the faces of men and women as evening approaches, and bad weather...'

A pile of matter, a mechanical chaos, a little Babel: that is the city in daylight.

No, now it is something else: the place where you stand... It is consciousness, an independent and spacious form, it is a vehicle that transports the inheritance of night and day through endless zones.

The brightness of glass

All around the city, in market-places, squares and on street-corners, small towers have been erected. I look at them for my delight; they please my restless eye.

If I were asked to describe them, I would say they were green. Yes, they are the same green as the trams and the rubbish-bins in the park. But their walls are, for the most part, of window-glass. They can be seen far away, for lights always burn within them, and there is no lock on their door, but only a handle, so anyone can step inside at any time.

I have even seen queues in front of these towers in the evenings, after the office day is over. I have seen people step inside alone, money in their hand, and the heavy door closing automatically behind them. For two, such a tower is cramped, and yet it is built as a meeting-place, made for dialogue.

But an anonymous rage is directed at these narrow glass rooms. Cracks like stars have been made in the glass walls, and often I have had to return home without success: it is not possible to make contact.

But, for me, these towers are as beautiful as Chinese pagodas. The greatest publicity combines, in them, with the greatest privacy.

He who has entered can be watched by anyone who remains outside in the darkness of evening. I can see him through the glass as clearly as in underwater light. I see a finger picking one number after another from a disc, and thereby choosing its own route.

The profile of his face does not move; it lingers in its own peace like a statue. Inside the tower is a quiet pool in the current.

But he who has stepped inside the tower has been able to

go still further. I can see him there, it is true, but he himself is already elsewhere, in the place where he sends his voice. I see his lips opening, and, impatient in my waiting, I feel envious that he has already arrived.

At night, these small green towers are the lighthouses of the city. In their glass-bright isolation, their transparent solitude, they bear witness to the reality of contact.

When I was ill, I dreamed of a small glass house like that, just that and nothing else. All through the dream, nothing moved; the dream itself was an empty, green cell that made a sound. It called incessantly, reverberating as if it were ringing out in a very open space, in a night-time station hall or the depths of the past.

But there was no one to answer it, for although it was I who dreamed the dream, I was not there either.

Doña Quixote

Whenever someone whines that miserable expression, 'That's life', and nods his head with kindly condescension, I remember Doña Quixote. I see her narrow white fist pounding the table so that the ashtray dances and hear her passionate contradiction, made with all her strength: 'No! That's not life! That's not life at all, unless you make it like that yourself...'

How tall and thin she is. Sometimes it seems to me that she is constantly growing, not in the same way as children, but as if a reaction to gravity were constantly trying to pluck her free of the ground.

I am always shocked when I look at her ankles and her wrists. I am amazed when I see her feet. How can she stay upright and go forward on such thin ankles and such narrow feet?

One night I see her from behind as she stands in front of a window, and I start. For it seems as if there were a tree in the room.

Doña Quixote says herself that she is not a person. I am inclined to believe her. But it could also be that it is the other way round: she is so much more a person than people generally that it is for that reason she seems peculiar.

But Doña Quixote is not the knight of the sorrowful countenance. When I think of her like this, from a distance, her shape is that of a flame, and I would like to stretch out my finger to warm it at her blaze.

I am not the only one who has the same desire. In the evenings, her little room is often full of chilly people. They arrive one by one and look askance at one another; each of them believes each of the others to be an interloper.

Indeed, I have never met so many unhappy people as at

Doña Quixote's house. Their unhappinesses are different, but all of them are alone and all of them believe they have fallen from the tree of life. Their lamentation echoes and multiplies as they bump into obstacles, and the obstacles are other people.

Doña Quixote is the only person it does not affect. She allows it to pass through her, and it sinks into the shade of the valley of silence, so that they may forget.

But Doña Quixote's visitors often change. This year one no longer sees the same faces as last year. Where do they all go?

Sometimes it so happens that they meet Doña Quixote in the street and no longer recognise her. I have seen Doña Quixote greet them, even take hold of their coat-sleeves, but they look at her with such puzzlement that she becomes embarrassed and lets them go.

'Why do they forget you so quickly?' I ask, unhappily.

She thinks. Her violet gaze comes from an unimaginable distance.

'If they remembered me, they would remember their unhappiness,' she says.

The procession

As a child, Doña Quixote once went into her parents' bedroom when there was no one there and the rest of the family was listening to the radio in the living room.

Doña Quixote went up to her mother's dressing-table; she wanted to see herself. But when she looked in the mirror, her reflection was not there. There were other people, quite unfamiliar, and many of them were wearing clothes she had not seen on anyone else: long cloaks, broad white collars, strangely shapped headdresses.

She looked and looked, and the people in the mirror, men, women and children, came and went in an unceasing procession.

'Won't it ever end?' wondered the small Doña Quixote before the mirror. She was tired, and she would have liked to see her own reflection, but the stream of strangers did not stop.

She saw them as though through a window, but did not know whether they could see her when she asked: 'When will it be my turn?'

'Did your turn ever come?' I ask Doña Quixote, who looks, in the light of the evening lamp, like an ancient Indian.

'It was my turn,' she said. 'That, precisely, is what my turn is; only time had to pass before I understood it.'

Uta and Ekkehart

Uta lived in another city a long time ago. By now she has been standing in the nave of the cathedral for seven centuries.

When I was a child, I got a postcard of Uta from Naumberg. I fixed the card to the wall in the hall with a drawing pin so that whenever I went out or came in, I saw Uta's delicate stone features.

Since then, I have seen other pictures of Uta. In one Uta is alone; in another her husband, Ekkehart, stands by her side. Between them, it seems to me, a deep and abiding silence intervenes.

Uta's cloak-wrapped form is proud and reserved. She holds the loose robe closed under her chin so that its collar rises almost in front of her mouth. For that reason I look at Uta's mouth almost furtively. It is like a pain that shames her, or a too intimate part of the body. It is tender and arrogant, a lovely wound, stubbornly forbidding.

Her right hand, which holds the robe, is invisible beneath it. But all the narrow fingers of the left hand are visible, slightly separated from one another. On her forefinger is a large, round ring, no doubt given her by Ekkehart. She has another jewel, too, in her otherwise simple attire: a buckle attached to the left shoulder of her robe, almost the same as on Ekkehart's broad chest.

Her hair cannot be seen: it is hidden by a helmet-shaped headdress surmounted by a lowish crown.

Her eyes look past you. Her lower lids are slightly narrowed, as if what she sees does not really please her. Quite right: a faint contempt sharpens Uta's gaze, so cloaked in tenderness and refinement that it is hardly recognisable.

Uta and Ekkehart. They are among the founders of the

cathedral of Naumberg, aristocrats of their city. The unknown master who sculpted Uta and Ekkehart had never seen them. When their portraits were completed, they had already been lying for decades in the crypt beneath this skyscraper, which was not built according to earthly dimensions.

Everything here is vertical as in a forest. But the glittering roses of the windows rise higher than the crowns of trees. There are no walls; only glass, pillars, ribs – only the fretwork of lath and staff, a thin line rising from octave to octave.

No, this is not a building, but a road raised up, a delirium knitted of stone, the megalomanic dream of a spider.

Little matter, more hope. And the higher the spears of the towers reach, the farther they banish what cannot be seen.

At their roots, in the midst of the strained pillars, a stone among stones, stands Uta. The evasion of her eyes, the collar raised to protect her face, the mouth that has been on the point of trembling for seven hundred years... Perhaps she would like to leave this place, withdraw into the shadows, decay and disintegrate into nothing.

Uta of Naumberg cathedral. Is there another statue which, in its unmoving stone, bears witness so incontrovertibly to the isolation of human flesh and the trembling of the spirit?

Cro Magnon boy

I cannot take my eyes off him, although I struggle to look past him at the bustle of the streets, the markets and the parks. He does not notice me, but I reflect him like a shiny surfacc.

He always gets on the bus at the same stop, by the school for deaf children. He has a striped, knitted cap on his head, like the ones all the other boys have, but the forehead beneath it is as if forged by some village idiot of a smith: where, in other people, it becomes concave as it approaches the root of the nose, in him it dashes crookedly forward and creases abruptly above his eyebrows. It is like a rain-shelter, a little visor, which he himself must also constantly be able to see.

He is followed by another, smaller boy, and they, too, are able to sit, because in the mornings the bus is half empty.

The language of his hands hypnotises me: elongated, lumpy fingers, as if contorted by rheumatism. The hands of an old goblin, but beautiful, passionately sensitive.

What are they saying? I do not understand anything, not a word, but I should like to know: it must be important. The little boy, who is sitting diagonally opposite me, hears and understands everything. They gesture, nod and laugh, and the smaller boy even drums on his knees. They do not notice the other passengers.

When I follow the signs he makes with his hands, I remember an Indian dancer who visited the city years ago. I was unhappy when I went to see her performance, and I was unhappy when the performance was over.

But in between, while I watched her body live as though it were not a human body but a flower's corolla, a flame, a beam of light, a lovely creature or something matter is perhaps intended to be, but that it always betrays and forgets – in between, as her brilliant sari fluttered and her wrists, her ankles, stretched, rose – I saw clearly that life, that joy . . .

And now, as the pantomime dwarf opposite me speaks in his strange tongue, silently and volubly, I seem to see again. . .

See, and forget once more. See, and forget.

The tower

Out walking one Sunday, Doña Quixote and I found ourselves in a park, at whose centre stood an old, red-brick tower. The tower was crenellated and its bricks glowed with a dry, rich warmth like that of earth in late summer.

Behind the tower, the park was split in two by a broad concrete road under which ran a traffic tunnel, but farther off on the slope grew some large maples. They were just changing colour; their green had already begun its long retreat.

'Come, let us sit in the shade,' Doña Quixote said. 'From here, we can see the pond.'

The pond was just a cataracted eye, muddy and overgrown. From it rose a mild breath of air, as from stale wine.

'In this park there was once a murder,' Doña Quixote said. 'I read about it in the paper a long time ago.'

'Who was killed?' I asked, playing with a maple leaf.

'A girl,' said Doña Quixote. 'She was raped and strangled by a boy she had never met before. Perhaps I would have forgotten that news item quickly if a certain phrase had not gone on echoing through my mind.'

I asked, since she remained silent.

'Don't hit me any more, I'm already dead,' Doña Quixote said.

'Look, a dragonfly!' I pointed at the long, blue needle that had alighted on Doña Quixote's sleeve.

Doña Quixote looked at the insect as it rested. On the harbour road a tram screeched; the dragonfly rose vertically into the air, remained motionless for a moment on the breeze and was gone.

Doña Quixote leaped up: 'Come, let's walk round the tower.'

We walked round the tower. It had eight sides and three floors and only one, tightly bolted, door. Who had built it, and for what purpose? We did not know. But it was part of the landscape as if it had grown there, as if it had roots. Doña Quixote strode ahead of me, tall and severe, like a tower herself.

'Shall we go?' I suggested, but she did not seem to hear.

'Do you know what she meant?' Doña Quixote said, and stood still.

'What?'

'By what she said, that girl. Have you heard small children playing hide-and-seek? Have you heard how a child will call to its seeker from its hiding place, "I'm not here"?'

And now the boy will always walk around this tower. It will always split his landscape in two.

'But don't you believe in something like reconciliation? Or if not reconciliation, then oblivion or – perhaps grace?'

But Doña Quixote did not answer, but beckoned with her finger to the dragonfly, which was quivering on her shoulder once more, on its wings the cold glimmer of scales.

The mummy

I have been travelling a long time to reach this town, where I have never been before and of whose language I speak only a few words. When the train arrives at the station, it is already evening, and my suitcase is heavy. I look on the platform for a porter, but instead a man in uniform steps up to me and gestures for me to follow him. When I hesitate, he shows me his card, from which it is clear he is a policeman or that, at any rate, he has a policeman's authority.

He takes me to the left luggage office and points to my bag. 'Open it,' he urges. I do so, and he examines and turns over everything I have, rummages through my socks, shakes the books and even opens a small box of chocolates.

'Why?' I ask, but he does not answer. Only when he unscrews my alarm clock do I realise he is looking for a bomb, and I also remember that just a short time ago, at a different station, an unsuccessful attempt at an assassination took place.

Well then, I do not have a bomb, and he pushes my bag toward me abruptly, without apology. But his unnecessary suspicion has already meant I have missed the bus in which I was to have continued to a nearby village to a family I know. The first boarding house I find is full, and in the second I discover there is a big trade fair in the city.

I walk up one street and down another, dragging my suitcase, which does not contain a bomb, and peering at hotel signs. The streets are flooded with people, but I cannot even hope to see any familiar faces. In a cramped and dark reception I am finally handed a small key, for a sum that is unreasonable.

When I open the door, I see the room is already inhabited: in the other bed lies someone wrapped in blankets, turned to the wall and apparently fast asleep. This does not please me; I have paid for a single room and feel I have been cheated. But I am tired; I do not have the energy to go downstairs again and object in a foreign language.

On the back wall is a tall mirrored wardrobe; I see myself on the threshold, as unremarkable as anyone else in the bustle of the street. I undress silently and quickly, so that my room-mate will not waken.

I lie awake for a long time in the room which does not belong to anyone, and whose objects exude the anonymity of all rooms that are only passed through. It is difficult for me to sleep, as I think of the many paths that have passed through this hole. It is difficult for me to fall asleep, as my room-mate is so motionless and her breathing so light that I can hardly distinguish it in the small quiet spaces of my own breathing.

I do not believe she is sleeping.

When I awake, I know I have been sleeping. Someone is crying as if she has been crying for a long time, many hours hiccuping and panting. The bed below the window is shaken by violent convulsions of grief.

I listen to these eruptions of emotion tensely, thinking I should really get up and ask: 'What is it?'

I stir, shift, and begin to lift the coverlet, but she seems to understand my intention and attempts to stifle her moans. I cannot decide: I lie for a long time in the darkness without a cover, and I grow cold. The stifled groans swell once more, sighs take the space and the air from the room, and the stranger's tears moisten my own life, too, with their bitter rain.

Endless weeping! Limitless grief! It gushes like a hot geyser from the chasm in that unknown life, so deep that it does not seem possible to find enough to fill it anywhere, it erupts as lava that reaches and petrifies all movement. The ebb and flow of the sobbing rocks my bed, and her tears combine with the sombre waters of my memory so that, with horror, I too feel them begin to surge.

No, I do not want to remember, I say to myself. But what good is it? My memory is that sheet-wrapped mummy.

And as I struggle in the darkness to bar the door to the procession of humiliation and disappointment, regret and shame, bitterness and misunderstanding, fear and loss, it rises, the thing that was still, a moment ago, the grief of my faceless room-mate, rises as high as Hokusai's wave, and I hear the thundering I know has always, incessantly, sounded around my mean, closed, dry life.

Mozart cheated us!

In November a desperate man came to see Doña Quixote. He said his innards were scorched by a hatred so bitter it would be enough to burn the entire city to ruins. He said it smoked in his brain just as phosphorus can smoulder in still-living flesh.

'Water does not quench phosphorus,' was what he said, 'and no comfort can easy my wrath.'

On Doña Quixote's table was a record sleeve, and as he spoke the man took it in his hand and turned it with restless fingers. It was Mozart's *The Magic Flute*.

'Wolfgang Amadeus Mozart!' said the man, and his voice crackled like rifle-fire. 'Wolfgang Amadeus Mozart!' he cried a second time, in the manner in which a court usher calls the name of the accused who is to appear before the judge.

'He is a liar,' the man said. 'Wolfgang Amadeus Mozart cheated us.'

'How did he cheat us?' asked Doña Quixote, calmly.

The man laughed bitterly. 'Because he deceives us into believing things that don't exist. Just remember the clarity of his string quintets, the *Magic Flute*'s noble ideal of brotherhood and Tamino's unselfish love or the delight of the glockenspiel... There is nothing like that to be found in the world, and he must have known it himself.'

'But,' said Doña Quixote mildly, 'he also has the Dies irae and the Ave verum corpus.'

'Yes,' the man conceded. 'They are his, and they are the world's. Everything else is sweet deception, the empty chiming of a glockenspiel.'

The table jolted, and the man drew back, startled. Doña Quixote, who had pounded her fragile fist down in front of him, looked at him with blazing eyes.

'Do you think,' said Doña Quixote, low and *maestoso*, 'do you really think he was unable to see beyond the days of wrath, dizzyingly far, as far as here, and still further? You think you can't survive. How long has Mozart survived?'

The man sat in silence for a long while. He seemed to have calmed down, and after a time began to speak of something quite different.

As he left, and was already bidding us good night, he lingered on the threshold. I felt he intended to say something important, but he merely commented, 'The weather is easing,' put his cap on his head and left.

'Hell's revenge burns within my heart,' muttered Doña Quixote after he had gone. 'Do you know who he was? He was the Moor, Monostatos.'

And then she hummed: 'Das klinget so herrlich, das klinget so schön...'

The room of change

All rooms move. Each of them swings in a pendulum motion between evening and morning, moving its inhabitants closer to the unknown land where they will be no more.

But this room wanders through the streets, and the inhabitants within are constantly changing. Whenever it stands still, someone leaves and others take his place and they seek a space for themselves among the crowd of evasive eyes.

When I was a child, I saw them differently. I saw them there, at the door, as they paused for a moment before they made their exit, holding a pole under a sign which read: 'Do not stand in front of the mirror.' I only had to narrow my eyes a little and I could see them as they had once been, to narrow them again, and on their faces was the satiety of age.

I no longer see in this way. Now I am one of them and, like them, I take my place by the windows to see all that is already familiar to me: lights and signs, arrows and numbers, the swarming of overcoats and the dusty herds of the roads – and all of it flows past my tepid gaze, bordered by kerbstones, in a dense torrent.

I remember the experiments I used to conduct in this room. How I tried to tame Time and always failed. How I examined how long 'now' lasted, and how long its memory, how I stretched it like chewing-gum and, when it snapped, how I became tired.

My patience was not sufficiently great. My attention not sufficiently concentrated. The knife of a new event always came to cut time in two. It was a divided reality, and I learned that there, in the room of change.

This room has its route and its timetable. But the contents of the room change, and with them everything.

I have seen, here, a man who arranged the cities of Germany on the thin thread of his memory, I have heard how he dropped their names like coins into a box: Aachen, Augsburg, Berlin, Bonn…

Wherever he comes from, there is no hope. Wherever he goes, there is nothing to be done. But those tiny pieces of knowledge he presses upon one: like a torn entrance ticket to something, a party that has already been held or cancelled…

And we sit or stand in our places and nevetheless we glide forward. This oblong, lighted trunk that moves, all these forgotten heads at the windows…

Sometimes in the street, at rush-hour, when the city bus drives past me, crammed full, I feel like laughing. What a sight! Just as strange as if a swarm of witches were riding on a broom above the city lights…

Onward it rushes, always on time, always on its route, and its windows are entirely covered in frost or condensation, people's breathing.

Onward it rushes, past withering parks and windows just lighting up, and its cargo is the weight of many displaced souls.

The room of time

Tick-tock.

Some clocks really did make that noise. But most of them were silent: inside them was a battery made them keep time for a year, two years, or even eight.

We had gone to the clock-shop, for the strap of Doña Quixote's watch had broken. The clock-shop was very small, and strange in that it contained more ugly objects than I had ever before seen together.

On the highest shelf were arranged, in order of size, a row of bronze-coloured goblets that recalled women constricted by corsets.

'If I were a competitor,' I thought, 'and could see a trophy like that in advance, I would want to lose.'

On the walls hung pocket-watches on plastic chains decorated with turquoise and aniline-red spirals. There were ashtrays, too, in the form of riding-boots, mouths and lavatory bowls. But everything was covered in a thin, greasy dust, as if no customer had been here for weeks.

'Good morning,' says Doña Quixote.

'Morning,' says the clock-seller, and rises behind the counter, barrel-like and bloody-eyed, as strange as the things with which he has surrounded himself.

He shows Doña Quixote watch-straps and photograph-frames sprinkled with gold-dust. They do not make an impression on Doña Quixote.

She is looking at the digital watches under the glass.

'They have no faces. They do not show time, they show the moment. There is no day or night for them. They have no history, do they have a future?

The clock-maker ponders, and I shift my weight from one

foot to the other, looking at a plaque of juniper-wood. On it is branded: 'One cannot keep house in cloud, in wind.'

'I think people have already got bored with them,' says the clock-seller. 'They don't buy as many digital watches as before.'

'What is time, really?' says Doña Quixote.

'What?' asks the clock-seller.

'Time is matter,' explains Doña Quixote. 'Yes, it is matter and, furthermore, elastic. A kind of wax.'

'Ah...'

'If you really want to,' Doña Quixote says, 'you can learn to model it. Stretch it like chewing gum. Roll it into a pretty little ball. Throw it away, except that it is a boomerang. It comes back.'

And Doña Quixote leans on the counter and the countless clocks as if it is she, in fact, who has to try to sell them.

'Last summer I happened to be there when the city stood still. Smoke sat motionless above the roofs. There in the street, a cyclist pedalled and pedalled, but got nowhere. The traffic lights stuck at red and the bells of St John's church could only ring, "ding, ding, ding"...'

'Give me that,' she says next, and points to a watch-strap.

The clock-merchant hurries to try it on her stick-thin wrist, and after that he has to go into the back room, where he makes a new hole in the strap. He is extremely polite, hurries to open the outer door and, on the threshold, thrusts his card into Doña Quixote's hand.

On the journey home, Doña Quixote is quiet and anxious-looking.

'Do I look old?' she suddenly asks.

I deny it quickly.

'You're lying,' she says cruelly. 'I looked in the window and saw for myself. I do look old.'

'What window do you mean?'

'The clock-shop,' she said. 'I saw my head there among all those dreadful things, and it was very old.'

I say no more, and she would not listen if I did. She stops in the middle of the pavement, and her face is naked, and tired.

'Time is a tiger,' she says. 'It has no morals. None!'

Then she strides forth again, so it is hard for me to keep up with her. At the crossroads where we have to part, she grasps my arm and smiles mysteriously.

'Do you know what it is that is unaffected by time? Do you?'

Her eyes have the glimmer of valleys at evening.

I shake my head, and she whispers, 'It's the twinkling of an eye, do you believe me?'

Patroclus, too, is dead

On a bright, ringing frosty day I meet, at Doña Quixote's house, the Incurable One. It is as if the city has been dusted with icing-sugar; a glittering layer of snow-dust has frozen to the walls and the branches of the trees.

The Incurable One is sitting in Doña Quixote's uncomfortable armchair, as pale as if he, too, were made of snow.

Once he used to come here often, but now he spends long periods in hospital, and movement has become increasingly difficult for him. Seven years ago his daughter died in a car crash, and soon afterwards his wife departed.

But now he sits by Doña Quixote's window, and the February light casts blue lines of shadow across his forehead and neck. He sits almost touching the radiator, but he seems to exude a coldness its warmth cannot reach.

Doña Quixote and the Incurable One are talking about birds. Birds are the Incurable One's great love, but he says it is years since he has seen the spring or autumn migrations.

Doña Quixote says that one night, when she was walking along her own street, a barn owl flew out of the garden porch.

'It flew low and soundlessly,' said Doña Quixote. 'And as it passed us, it looked straight into my eyes.'

'Owls can hypnotise you,' said the Incurable One, and nodded.

He glanced at the high sky and sighed. 'Spring is coming. I should like to see the birds return once more.'

'They will fly again,' said Doña Quixote.

The Incurable One rose with difficulty, fetched his briefcase from the hall, and pulled out a large book.

'"Dear friend",' he read, '"you too must die, why do you complain so? Patroclus is dead, and he was a far better man than you. Death and a cheerless fate threaten me, too. There will come some morning, or evening or noon, when someone will destroy my life in battle…".'

He read with a weak but vital voice, and the words that he left in the room rang as crystal-cold as the February day.

In April I rang on Doña Quixote's door. When she opened it, still on the threshold, she said: 'Patroclus is dead.'

We went to walk on the shore. It was a day when everything was breaking and melting, vanishing and lifting, the kind of day when all that is old seems to be disappearing and there is not yet anything new to take its place.

'It said in the paper,' said Doña Quixote, 'that the lark has already arrived.'

I looked up, but the sky was low and without gaps. It was like a broad and downy wing.

'Do you hear?' Doña Quixote said, but I could hear nothing.

'Everything here is beneath it. So that when someone dies, someone else can go on singing…'

The sun-cypress

In this city there is a landscape that I often watch and that is not changed by the seasons. I do not have to climb a panoramic tower, walk to the shore or even look out of the window.

This landscape is here, in my own room. No one who steps inside can fail to see the island or the evergreen tree on a hillock on the island.

My island is a flower-pot whose earth has been gathered into a mound, round as a breast, and the tree is a bonsai tree, a small sun-cypress.

This tree is very old. Its trunk is twisted and warped as if it had grown in the grip of storms on a skerry far out at sea. But this is not so; the free winds of the sky have never tossed its needles, although it has already lived a human life-span or two. It has been grown through torture, in a handful of poor earth, through pruning, binding and pinching.

Its bent shape contains the spirit of all the points of the compass.

In the shadow beneath the tree grow some low shoots. When I return from the city, I wish I could throw myself there, into the shade of the tree, on my back among the brown shoots.

I would like to stay there until evening to see, just to see how silver-green the needles are, and how rough the bark of the trunk.

And when the August evening, as summer breaks into autumn, lights up the city sky, this sun-cypress is, against the glimmer, black as a calligraphic sign drawn by a master.

If I could – if I had to interpret its message, I would content myself with repeating the words of Sonya Alexandrovna:

'You have not been able in your life to feel joy, but wait – – – wait... Then we shall have rest... Then we shall have rest.'

The peacock

'Are you sure?' I asked. 'I thought peacocks existed only in the zoo.'

'How could anyone be mistaken about a peacock?' she asked in turn. 'Especially if you see it spread its tail.'

We were sitting in a café and she was looking at her inverted mirror image in the concave surface of a teaspoon.

'I think I waited for my husband until three in the morning. I couldn't wait any longer; I had to go out.'

I had no idea where to look for him, but I stopped a passing taxi and asked it to drive to the city centre. Just as I had paid and was stepping out on to the pavement, the street-lamps went out. I walked down to the bar and saw it was shut. I walked to the street corner and crossed at the crossing where the traffic lights were blinking orange. I met no one, and I saw that everywhere was closed.

I turned to walk back; I had no more money.

I took a short cut across the old allotment gardens. I followed a lane bordered by palings and hedges of hawthorn and white-painted wooden gates. Many of the gates were decorated by the figure of a sun, whether rising or setting I could not say.

Behind the fences were clapboard cabins in yellow, red and green, fantastically small and neat with their white cornices. The sky lightened, and the edge of the real sun rose far beyond the tower blocks of the suburbs.

The apple-trees were shedding their last blossoms, and my anguish was greater than my fatigue. I saw my husband dead, I saw him with another.

Then I heard from my left side, behind the fence, a high-pitched screech. I turned and saw a peacock strutting along under the gnarled apple tree. It was green and silken blue and it was dragging its tail through the morning dew on the grass.

I saw it, and perhaps it had been watching me for a long time. We stood there, facing one another, between us the white fence, and at the same moment it puffed itself up, it stretched its neck, shook itself along the whole of its length, jumped a short step backward and spread its tail to its full breadth, and it rocked and shimmered its fan of glossy colour before me, its living rainbow, its eye-fringed flower of paradise, and all the time, above it, flakes of apple blossom were scattering.

Night and the other

There came nights when one of them fell out of his bed as if it had bounced upright and thrown him to the ground in a calculated full-nelson. And just before the thud a toneless 'Help!' was torn from his throat, the kind of wheeze one could imagine coming from a paralysed person whose bedclothes had caught fire.

In her own bed, the other started upright and mumbled, 'It was only a dream', while he crept back on to his mattress, turning his back like a barrier.

But it was not a dream. It was the life they shared, which was dying and was crying out with the mouth of one of them. Which could not escape their mercilessness, their rancid love, their regret or their vengeance.

Now one slept while the other lay awake. She who lay awake had waited throughout a long evening. And the other one had come back, certainly, but what she had been waiting for did not return, and would not return any more, if it had ever even existed. But the waiting continued, as a thirst that parched like the sirocco.

Now, in this darkness, the expression had been wiped away, the expression that was so strange to her face but was attempting to conquer it: winsome, knowing its defeat in advance and therefore suffering, and therefore so deeply repugnant. Night had peeled it from her face like the dough from which the bread of separation and contempt is baked.

Bathed by the night, her face, which no one could see, lay on the stains of the pillowcase like a bitter flower, turned toward the darkness of the ceiling. Her body, which was already beginning to abandon the memories and demands of love, was hers alone; it was a light and redundant thing, unstirring and clearly delineated, drawn on the bed as the shapes of the figures lying in coffins were once drawn on their lids.

But from this reed, she knew, there could now, at last, burst a voice, a voice she had long yearned to hear, a voice that spoke with heartfelt compassion like an ample nanny, a question that was tender and dark, an answer that was convincing, firm and joyful: 'Why thus? For you do not need to live like this... Whatever is crooked, make straight. Whatever is spoiled, throw away. Whatever is dead, bury.'

She could hear the other's breathing and she breathed like his dream; the same wind passed in and out of their nostrils. The same wind – and she was astonished: how had it come into the room?

She was no longer thirsty, and she knew the waiting was over. A wave had submersed their room and had arrived, in the night, at the point where the waiting ended.

She considered getting up and going over to the other, waking him and saying: 'It is here now.'

But she did not get up before it was morning.

The chamber

In late autumn, when the weather changes, Doña Quixote becomes restless. It is as if she begins to flicker, and from time to time her mood turns round like a leaf twirled by the wind.

Today she says she must move out of her chamber. Her 'chamber' – that is what she calls her apartment, and the word echoes in her mouth like a vault.

'Where would you go?' I ask.

'It's impossible to live here,' she says, not answering. 'People have left their unhappiness here. This is not an apartment, but a rubbish tip. This chamber stinks.'

Then she digs out Sunday's newspaper from somewhere and begins to examine the section headed Property: Apartments.

Later, we are standing in an unfamiliar hall and an estate agent is thrusting leaflets into our hands. We look at the plan of the flat: a room, a kitchen alcove, a bathroom and three built-in wardrobes.

The room is empty and naked. It is the abstraction of a room, it is any space at all, a cube full of emptiness.

There is the door, through which one can go in and out. There is the window, from which one can see. It gathers light from the winter sky and scatters it into this empty vessel.

The estate agent speaks of the floor-covering, the tiles, and of the respectability of the residents.

'If you lived here,' I say to Doña Quixote, 'what would be different?'

She does not answer, but opens a cupboard door. I do not see anything but a clothes-rail, but she remains gazing at it for a long moment.

'If you moved here,' I ask again, 'do you suppose your memories would not move with you?'

She gazes on at the cupboard, and I cannot even guess what she is thinking.

'"And if sadness were to strike you here..."'

'Be quiet!' she says, and slams the cupboard door shut. Then, cheerfully: 'Come!'

She marches along the pavement, whistling. I rush after her, up one street and down another, to the left, right, left, and then a couple of steps forward. The slush spatters around our feet; the shop windows are framed by garlands of spruce. The wind blows through us, through the whole city, and Doña Quixote's gaze is fixed on a distant spot.

'Do you know this?'

She whistles something like a question into the fog of the street light.

'What is it?'

'Pong pontuli, pong pongtuli,' she hums, and extracts a key from her pocket.

I look at the tuft of grass that swayed all summer in the cleft in the stone step outside Doña Quixote's front door. Now it is only yellowed straw, but to me it still looks as if it split the stone.

After we have returned to the Chamber, Doña Quixote pulls on a robe made out of some kind of hempen fabric whose elbows are worn through, and prepares a herbal drink for herself. She claims it improves her sight.

No, there is no smell of unhappiness here, only tobacco and the dust of books. On the window-sill are stones from the shore and a Samos goblet. If you fill it to the brim, the drink flows away to the very last drop. Lost in thought, I often turn it over in my hands.

'For mankind, nothing is ever enough,' said Doña Quixote once, when I asked the meaning of the clay goblet.

'He asks for more, more and more. And then – oops! – he loses what he already had.'

That is the lesson of the goblet of moderation.

The poplars

In the breaks between lessons, the girls walked under the poplars, arms linked. They wore pleated terylene skirts, and petticoats stiffened with foam rubber. When they moved, it sounded as though they were wading through dry leaves.

Which of them ever looked at the poplars? Constantly present but nevertheless strangers, they took part in the girls' lives by dropping shadows into the gulf of the yard, and pale green catkins, and their shrivelled leaves as messages about the great autumn that, from one spring to the next, came closer to them: in the branches that no longer made new shoots.

Among the babbling of the yard, the air was often pierced by a vulgar, high-pitched laugh. It was Deska, who had twice had to repeat a year, and was already a woman.

Sometimes she went up to Anttila, under the bare branches. The sky glittered like new aluminium, and Deska was wearing around her neck a silk scarf with blue waves.

'Do you know why I have this scarf?' she asked Anttila.

'Because it is beautiful,' said Anttila. 'Because you were given it as a present. Or else you have a sore throat.'

'No no no,' said Deska. 'Look!'

She pulled the scarf and the neck-opening of her pullover down over one of her shoulders so that Anttila had a long glimpse of her pale, almost luminescent, skin, and then a little bruise, about the size of a small coin.

Anttila examined it, screwing up his eyes, but his gaze soon rose to meet Deska's. They came to his expectant, shining, demanding.

'Where did you get that?' Anttila asked. 'Did you fall?'

'Pooh!'

The impatient finality with which Deska pulled the scarf back into its place.

'Don't you understand,' she said. 'It's called a love-bite.'

'What?'

'A love-bite,' she said. 'Do you want me to spell it for you?'

The scarf with the blue waves bobbed far off in the forbidden gateway. There was a rustling as the girls walked, arm in arm, back and forth, back and forth, but the leaves had been swept off the asphalt long ago.

A spring evening

A friend whom I had not seen for two years had returned to the city.

I had laid the table and prepared a meal. When we had sat down, we looked at each other over the freesias he had brought.

It was early spring.

We wanted to tell each other everything, absolutely everything that had happened during the time we had been apart. And we did. The spring evening darkened outside and we drank another glass of wine. I lit a candle, and we spoke more softly, and with lengthening pauses.

It was so peaceful. My apartment was a home once more. The plates emptied, and I carried them into the kitchen. When I returned, he looked at me curiously and for a long time. I sat down again opposite him, sipped my drink and nodded to him, but it was difficult for me to follow his speech and my thoughts had begun to wander.

When I tried to concentrate once more on him and the moment at hand, I suddenly had the impression something decisive had changed. Perhaps it was something in his face, or tone of voice: its timbre was now different.

I stroked my hair. I touched my eyebrows. I shook the crumbs from the front of my blouse. From time to time he eyed me as if something in my appearance disturbed him.

'Would you like a cup of coffee?' I asked but he refused, abruptly and without explanation. The harshness of his refusal embarrassed me, so that after a pause, which seemed very long, I was unable to begin the conversation again.

When, at last, I began hurriedly to speak, he spoke a sentence at the same time, which I did not catch.

'Sorry,' I said, and he: 'No, after you.'

But I had already forgotten what it was I had intended to say.

I wanted to turn on the standard lamp, but it was behind him, and I could not get up and cross the floor while he watched. I heard him start to speak again, but his sentences were fragmented, and indeed I could now understand hardly a word he spoke. I do not know whether the fault was in him or in my own capacity to understand, or in the space of air between us, which had rapidly thickened and darkened.

He stammered a little, and it seemed to me that he was avoiding looking directly at me. This was so, there was no doubt about it: his gaze only grazed my shoulder, and he turned more and more often toward the darkness of the window so that I could see only his cheek as it grew dim in the candlelight.

Then I gathered my strength and sat down so he could not – so I imagined – avoid looking me in the eyes. But I was wrong: he merely glanced in my direction and, without hesitation – it was unexpected, after all! – moved his chair so that he was sitting with his back completely turned to me.

The strength flowed from my limbs and I began to swallow. Neither of us was speaking any longer. There was no use pretending. I could hear him breathing quickly and unevenly, but his back was very straight. Expectation made me tremble so that a faint creaking could be heard from the joints of my chair.

I could not help it: a little hiccup rose from my throat, and then he leaped up, pushing his chair to one side. I raised my arm in front of my eyes and the chair fell.

Footsteps resounded – he had gone.

The memory of our deeds

One night in winter I was sitting in Doña Quixote's apartment reading a magazine. I felt her eyes on me and raised my head.

'Tell me who you are,' she said slowly.

It was an aggravating question. I wished she had not asked it.

'I have thought about it,' I said, 'but it is something that does not become clear. I only know that if I look at something for a long time, anything at all, I begin to resemble it like a sister. And I know what I would have liked to have been.'

'What?' asked Doña Quixote.

'A pair of blue eyes, that and nothing else,' I said. 'I would have liked always to stay on the auditorium side, because it is dark there, it is quiet there, there nothing ever happens. Only eyes move... But I came to understand that no one is allowed to stay there, no one at all.'

'Because there is no such thing as the auditorium side,' Doña Quixote said. 'Because the world bathes in the limelight of the sun and moon. And everyone has to be Hamlet, is that what you mean?'

'The memory of our deeds... "When we awake, only the memory of our deeds remains".' That line now came back to me.

'It is not a good line,' Doña Quixote said.

'I don't know,' I said. 'But it is my life's line.'

'Because you live inside your head,' said Doña Quixote. 'It is the sentence of those who live inside their head.'

She knocked on my hairline with her cool and slender finger.

'Hey, come out of there,' she ordered.

'Where?' I asked.

'There you are,' said Doña Quixote, and leaned back, satisfied. 'You do understand, after all.'

'Do I?' I asked, astonished.

'That you're already outside. In the wide world. Sometimes people just forget. And then there is nothing but themselves and the memory of their deeds.'

The Looking-Glass Boy

I do not know why Doña Quixote calls him the Looking-Glass Boy. I asked her once, but she did not answer.

Everything changes quickly in the mirror of his face. It is small and glowing like a focus. He is as full of eyes as an archangel.

Unceasingly, even in his sleep, he is growing.

'Aren't you finished yet?' I say to him often. 'I think that is exactly the right size. The best size of all.'

But he does not stop.

Sometimes I catch him in my arms and press my ear against his chest. Will I hear more than the light paces of his heart? The sound of growth, the song that once murmured in every body? It is like the ceaseless rushing of a waterfall or an invisible radiation and it surrounds everything that grows.

'Trilzadam qwalamba. Weedoo! Sorozzo!'

'What's that? But what is it, really?' I keep asking, and he comes right up to me and repeats: 'Tril-za-dam qwa-lam-ba. Wee-doo! So-roz-zo!'

And I still understand nothing, and he laughs.

Once I had an idea that I would teach him. I said: 'People are born and grow, grow old and die.'

How angry he became! He stamped his feet and shouted: 'It's not like that! It's not like that!'

'How is it, then?' I asked, astonished.

'No one ever dies!' he said, and looked at me with condescension.

In the spring we flew a kite from the boulders on the shore. Oh dear, it escaped from his hands and the wind took it out over the open sea. It was a hawk, black and blue, and the cold waves fought over its wings.

He did not cry.

Now the first snows have fallen and the city glows with the distant light of winter.

The tall stone building is empty. Everyone has gone; I don't know whether to work or to the shops, on journeys or to death.

Only the Looking-Glass Boy plays in the chasm of the yard, in the shadows of the snow. I see from my window how the flakes fall on his brightly coloured cap and on the cellar steps and on the frost of the sandpit. With what infinite humility they fall on to brick and metal, wood and glass, concrete and human hands.

I shout his name and he looks up, bends over and scoops up some snow. His fingers are bare.

'Catch!'

He throws it toward the light of the window. The severe substance of eternity and the warmth of his fingers, transparent.

Sometimes he has rested beside me and I have believed he was sleeping. But his eyes are open, after all, and he looks through me as through a window.

'When I fall asleep,' he said later, 'or when I wake, all the colours come here.'

'Where from?' I ask, and he points to the white wall on which the door, slightly open, has drawn a glowing pillar.

What could ease, what could ever dilute the ineluctibility of chance, that he has been born on earth.

The aquarium light

I have seen a small house in a forgotten quarter of the city. I call it the Gothic House because its roof slopes so steeply and the narrowness of its sides make it look so high that it recalls a dwarf cathedral.

I have never seen the people who live there, but I have been inside the house once. I had to go there on account of an aquarium, because a friend of mine, who knows the owners, had promised to look after the fish while they were away. One Sunday in May he rang and asked whether I wanted to go there with him. I did, for I would have gone anywhere at all with him.

'Here it is,' said my friend, opening a dilapidated door. It was already evening, and the slanting light cut across the long grass of the garden.

We entered a room that was cool and large.

'Wait a moment,' said my friend, and disappeared somewhere.

I found myself looking at a picture on the wall, and it was foreign to me. Someone was lying, eyes closed, in the middle of an open field. He was inside a low, transparent tent; perhaps it was some kind of mosquito net, made of gauze. The sleeper in the picture was surrounded by the dimness of a summer night; he lay on his back, his hands by his sides, like a dead person. But he was not dead, for the gauze, the room, all the summer night swayed with the breath of his sleeping.

In the darkest corner of the room stood the aquarium. I saw it only when my friend returned and switched on the lamp that was attached to the inside of its lid. I gazed into the small, water-filled room that glowed.

'What are you going to give them?' I asked.

'Mmm.' He studied the label of the jar of fish-food. 'These are freeze-dried termites.'

I opened the jar and inhaled; inside were small, dark crumbs that smelled of nothing. I was alert and carefree. I saw everything close up and in accurate detail.

The fish swam up close to the surface as soon as the light was switched on. I sprinkled the crumbs on the water, and their ring-mouths snapped. One of the fish was particularly large, greedy and beautiful.

'What's that?' I asked.

'Don't you recognise an ordinary goldfish?'

'Ordinary?'

Nothing that evening was ordinary. With what grace the creature moved; it had a shimmering, floating tail, a gold-glimmering veil, which fluttered slowly and artfully, as if the fish were a dancer.

'Do you think it can see us?'

'The odd movement, perhaps.'

The aerating device in the corner of the aquarium hummed unevenly; there was something in it of the wind and the sound of bells. The glow of the aquarium light struck the water and, from there, reflected into our faces as we leaned over the tank.

'Listen, about that trip,' my friend said. 'I don't think it's a good idea, after all.'

'How do you mean?' I asked. He was talking about a plan which we had been discussing for a long time: a visit to Assisi.

'I'll have to think about it some more.'

'Don't you want to go, after all?'

'That's not what I mean,' he said, absent-mindedly trailing his fingers in the water. The fish swam up to look at them, waving its tail, and the reflections of the water, stirred by its fins, marbled the skin of his cheeks like the glimmer of sunlight, as if we had been standing in the water of a river under a summer sky.

I wanted to ask: 'What do you mean?', to sort the matter

out straight away and in every detail. But speech had become an overwhelming exertion.

He lifted his fingertips and drops fell back into the underwater landscape, where reddish shells had been carefully placed and where thin reeds bent elegantly as if a wind were blowing.

'I'll just go and water the plants upstairs,' he said, and closed the lid of the aquarium.

'I'll wait here,' I said.

I watched his back as he went upstairs. From the small, black-and-white picture twilight poured into the room, spreading like a ring on water.

The beginning of spring spread itself before me, dazzlingly empty. It was a table spread with a spotless cloth, set with the empty dishes of weeks of lonely days.

The fish whisked its tail, and I wanted to say to him: 'You don't know me.'

'You don't know me.' How quickly I grasped, as my crutch, the secret comfort of all those who have been rejected: 'You don't know me. If you knew me, if you knew who I really am, you would love me forever.'

He returned, the empty watering-can in his hand, and eyed me carefully.

'I suppose I should turn off the aquarium light,' he said.

The remoteness of all glory

Doña Quixote is ill. I have never seen her so gloomy and ill.

I am in a hurry and I should have gone somewhere quite different. But I came here, nevertheless, knowing nothing of her state in advance.

Doña Quixote is lying between the sheets, wearing all her clothes. She has even left her shoes on her feet.

'I thought I would die last night,' she says.

'What happened?' I ask.

'I had such a bad nightmare,' she says, like a little child.

'Would you like some sage tea?' I ask.

She does not answer, and looks as if she is still gazing into her nightmare.

I make Doña Quixote some sage tea and she swallows a couple of gulps obediently. Then she pushes the cup away and says she wants to go away. Away completely. She says her strength has withered and crumbled. She says her eyes have grown dim. She says she has reached a place where all that is true is the remoteness of all glory.

Her words make me cold and my gaze avoids her eyes. I, too, am disappointed, as though my trust, my hope had been in vain.

I hear her sigh.

'I am growing tired,' she said, 'and so are you. And if it is for the last time, then let it be so. But whatever does not stir, remains.'

She sits on the edge of her bed and her long, white fingers hang like quills.

'Do you want to hear the dream that woke me up?'

'I do,' I said.

'It was very short,' Doña Quixote says. 'I was in a strange country, in a strange city. It was night. Around me were nothing but ruins. I saw hands, feet and heads that thrust their way out of the cracks between stones or lay, mutilated, on the pavement. They continued as far as the eye could see so I could no longer find a clear space to step on.'

She falls silent and stares with sightless eyes at a flower on her carpet. I take Doña Quixote's guitar from the corner and ask her to play something.

'Play "All the bright lanterns", for example,' I say.

But she does not touch the guitar.

'Whose dream did I dream?' she asks. 'Whose dream am I dreaming? Oh, how cold I am.'

I fetch a large blue shawl from the cupboard. I ask her to drink another cup of tea. I ask whether she would like to watch the television news, and when she continues to be silent, I turn the set on.

The television shows a strange city that has been bombed. The television shows a shanty-town that has been destroyed. The set shows men and women, girls and boys, all dead, all lying in the filth of the road, with snuffed-out faces.

A room of one's own

The peace of things. The comb that lies on the table before me between the pen and the book. The bottle of Aquila ink and a lump of blue glass I found on the beach at Murano. My gaze often moves over these things like a fly, understanding nothing of their purpose or origin.

Sometimes, on the other hand, when I look around me and see things that have been made and produced, sold and bought for money, I am astonished. Whence comes this persistent feeling that they are concealing a secret? That my room, although I know there is no one here but me, is inhabited by unknown people? That even the most insignificant object, such as a spent match or a crumpled bus-ticket, has its own, ineluctable personality, an individual life which must not be undervalued, a consciousness that has perhaps a more direct link with reality than the short feelers of the senses and language?

No, they do not conceal anything. Everything is here: visible and before me. Everything is precisely what it is, openly, every day. If reality has a secret, then it is this nakedness that is transparent.

The comb lies on the table before me between the pen and the book. How different they are from me, in that they have a purpose that I do not. But there are moments when our mutual understanding is unbroken. The great expectation we hold in common.

I understand the psychometrist who, taking an object in his hand, can say where it has come from and who has used it. For cannot crumbs from a loaf of bread prove who ate the bread? The handle of a cup I once grasped will carry forever the wavy lines of the epidermis of my forefinger and thumb...

The empty room

'Nothing exists,' said the Looking-Glass Boy.

He has come into my room and his finger turns toward my table.

'Hey,' I shout, 'I still have a lot of work to do.'

He does not seem to hear. He has already managed to say it: 'The table does not exist.'

Then he looks at the painting I have hung on the wall. It is a beautiful picture. I have grown used to it, and I like to look at it.

'Listen,' I begin, but his finger is already pointing straight at it. 'The picture does not exist.'

This depresses me a little. I would like to sit down, but when I look round I see the Looking-Glass Boy has already pointed at my chair.

And it was a good chair. I had been sitting in it for many years.

'I don't want to sleep on the floor,' I tell him severely, but it is no use. If nothing exists, why should he spare the bed...

I see he has moved his gaze to my lamp.

'No,' I say, 'I want to see.'

But the lamp has already gone out.

So that now we are crouching in the darkness and there is nothing any more, anywhere, only we two.

But through the darkness I think I can make out something like a small stick...It is his pale, thin, beautiful finger.

Oh, I already know, I know!

It will turn slowly toward my heart, and there is nothing for me to use as my shield.

Lost

There are days when Doña Quixote ceases to speak.

When I step into the room, she sees my arrival, nods lightly and motions for me to sit. But when I ask something, she shakes her head, presses a finger to her lips, and her eyelids veil her gaze.

I say it is windy outside, and she smiles. I say I have brought us buns and cream for our coffee, and she looks at me tenderly but remains silent.

The blue and red mobile that she has hung on the curtain-rail spins slowly in the draught from the crack of the open window. On the table is an avocado whose furrowed skin is deep green, like late summer. I want to sit as silently as she, but I have travelled here from a great distance across the bustle of the city, and I have caught the restlessness of the streets.

There was something I absolutely had to tell her. What was it? What was it? I forget so much every time I step into this room.

When I look at Doña Quixote, she seems suddenly to have shrunk, as if the dimensions of the room had changed and there were dozens of yards between our chairs, as if she were already moving to the far side of where my voice can reach her.

I feel longing. I can no longer sit in one place, I get up and go to the kitchen to make coffee.

When I return, there is no sign of her. From the threshold, where I am standing, if I turn my head a little I can see the whole of the small room and the hall. I am sure I would have heard if she had gone out.

The bathroom door is ajar and it is dark inside: no one there. I tear open the alcove curtain, but she is not in her bed. A deep panic overwhelms me and I pull open the doors of all the cupboards and wardrobes. I rummage among her clothes as if she could have hidden herself among them.

I go into the alcove again and bend down to look under her bed. Do I really think I will see her irises there, in the dust and the darkness?

Then she speaks my name from the room behind me, low and gently. She is sitting beside the radiator in her own chair, in exactly the same position as when I got up and went into the kitchen to make coffee.

'Where were you?' I ask, angry now.

'I was here,' she says. 'But I've been sitting here all the time.'

'Be quiet,' I say. 'And don't do it again. It makes me ill.'

She smiles a little, and that makes me even angrier. I would like to say something hurtful to her as she sits there, so immovable and distant. I would like to say I shall never come here again, because she is – because she is – so thoroughly strange and different from everyone else. But when I even think of seeing her elongated form for the last time, hot grief flows like a liquid right out into my toes and my fingertips, and I sit down in my old place.

'Talk to me,' I say, 'and put an end to my trembling.'

I see her lips moving, I see she is speaking, but what she is saying I cannot hear. She talks and talks, but between us is something heavy and difficult. I struggle to understand, but I merely notice I am still afraid and that I do not recognise her whom I call Doña Quixote and who murmurs like a tree in a strange place.

Then she comes to me and strokes my hair.

Now I hear her say: 'It goes before me, and I can see the hem of its coat. And even were it to go through the gates of death, I must follow.'

'Doña Quixote,' I say, 'what are you talking about?'

'People lose everything,' she said. 'Knowledge and skill and all human abilities. Strength crumbles and beauty is snuffed out like a flame. Faith goes, and hope, and only one thing remains, the thing whose name I do not wish to repeat in vain.'

A tree stands before the window, the last ray of daylight encircles its trunk, which sways imperceptibly.

'One doesn't get used to living,' it says, as quietly and inwardly as if the wind had merely rustled its crown.

And I repeat, as swiftly as if its breathing had been transferred to me: 'That's how it is, one never gets used to living.'

A Gate Built in Water

It is perfectly true that, south from here, off the shore of a certain island, stands a Gate Built in Water.

I believe it has stood in the same place for many centuries. It is made of wood and, when some part of it rots, it is rebuilt exactly the same as it has always been.

I imagine the gate is so narrow that an oarsman must ship his oars to pass through it without difficulty.

I imagine it, because I have never seen the Gate Built in Water, and I do not wish to see it. The journey is too long, and even if I were to make it, I would prefer to stay in the hotel and draw the curtains.

But I have seen a picture of the Gate Built in Water, and I know the most important thing: it is beautiful. I remember it often and I am happy that it is there and remains there. I think if the island were overwhelmed by a natural disaster or by war, the surviving inhabitants would rebuild the Gate Built in Water before schools, shops and temples.

I hope it has no meaning. That whichever direction one chooses to pass through it, one goes nowhere. The water ripples around its pillars and they rise straight from the cold deeps and a dull sound is heard if they are touched by the blade of an oar.

Why would anyone sail through the Gate Built in Water? Why indeed, when one can sail past it just as well – and with far less trouble – on either side...

Nevertheless, wherever the Gate Built in Water is seen, everyone, at every time and in every place, will unquestionably go through it, and not only once, but again and again.

The measuring line of Zerubbabel

Doña Quixote, who was hanging half out of her window, reappeared completely in the room. I saw she had a pair of binoculars in her hand, and that she was for some reason agitated.

'That's what it is,' she muttered. 'Without a doubt.'

She passed me the binoculars and said: 'Look for yourself. There, there on the roof, do you see?'

Even with the naked eye it was easy to see that, far away, two men were climbing on a red tile roof. To me it did not look at all unusual; after all, there are chimney-sweeps, roof-menders, snow-shifters.

When I examined the two men through the binoculars, I saw they were connected by a long, pale rope, perhaps a measuring tape, which they were moving along the ridge of the roof.

The sight did not agitate me.

'It looks to me,' I said to Doña Quixote, 'as if they're measuring something. Probably the roof will be replaced soon.'

'Yes, they're measuring,' Doña Quixote conceded. 'That's exactly what they're doing. But I know more. For I know the name of their measuring tape.'

I was amazed.

'Do you? How could you know that?'

'Because I happened to read it this morning, just after I woke up. It is the measuring line of Zerubbabel.'

She fetched a black book from her book-case and began to read:

'And I lifted up my eyes and saw, and behold, a man with a measuring line in his hand!

'Then I said, "Where are you going?" And he said to me,

"To measure Jerusalem, to see what is its breadth and what is its length."

'And behold, the angel who talked with me came forward to meet him,

'And said to him, "Run, say to that young man, 'Jerusalem shall be inhabited as villages without walls, because of the multitude of men and cattle in it'."'

She read in a deep, carrying voice, and whenever she wanted to give a word a particular emphasis, she gave me a sharp look.

'"For who has despised the day of small things? They shall rejoice, and shall see the plummet in the hand of Zerubbabel. These seven are the eyes of the Lord, which range through the whole of the earth."'

She slammed the book shut.

'What do you say?'

'Well. It certainly is...'

'"It certainly is, it certainly is",' she mimicked. 'When will your ears open. And your eyes –'

'Is there something wrong with them, too?'

'You look at me with sceptical and cold eyes,' Doña Quixote said accusingly. 'The eyes of the world. Where have you hidden your own?'

'I don't know, yet, which are my own, Doña Quixote,' I said, a little ashamed. 'There are so many eyes. Many more than seven.'

'It is time to choose,' she said slowly. 'Truly, it is high time.'

'And what's more,' she flared up once more, 'don't come and talk to me about eyes.'

I fell silent.

'Not eyes,' she said, 'not eyes, but the seeing gaze...'

Her eyelids closed.

'How bright it is today! Today, today too, it is a day of small things... Look, can you still see Zerubbabel there?'

I got up to peer out of the window.

'No, he has gone.'

And Doña Quixote refused to speak any more of Zerubbabel.

When we went out to eat, it was already growing dark. In the last light, the light crescent moon was floating, and it had begun to freeze.

On the street we walked along almost all the windows were lit, just as in the street that ran across it, and in the square where the street ended. It looked as if the entire city, encircled by darkness, had stayed at home that night.

'There are so many people there, so many . . . ,' I seemed to hear Doña Quixote mutter as the ice on the puddles cracked under our shoes and one circle of light after another moved toward us.

Gold of Ophir

I will make men more rare than fine gold, and mankind than the gold of Ophir.

Isaiah 13:12

Serpula lacrymans

The weeping house

'Look!' I said, and raised my forefinger so that the others could see. A little cotton-wool-like foam had stuck to it. 'What on earth is this?'

We were cold although outside the sun was shining. It was August, the rotten month. That day, I and Mrs Raa and Latona, the daughter of Pontanus, saw the Tabernacle once more. It was empty now the Gold-Washers were gone.

The pavilion had burned or been burnt, but the main building looked, on the surface, unchanged, as solitary as before and ready for flight with its wings, its pillars and its domed roof.

Like vandals, we had broken a pane, although it was already cracked, and climbed in through the window. We wondered why the glass was misty, as though people had been bathing or boiling water inside. The high skies of August were forgotten behind the panes. We stood in the Pantheon, and the great circular hall from which doors opened to all the rooms of the ground floor echoed our presence.

The statues were still there. The full-scale wooden caricatures lurked in their wall-cupboards in the positions I remembered. But they looked mouldy and blackened, as if they had been abandoned under the empty sky to the mercy of innumerable hard winters.

And when we looked around us, I and Mrs Raa and Latona, the daughter of Pontanus, we were still more astonished. The floor beneath our feet, the curving walls, the high roof – why did they look like that? So dark, so damp, so cold... For it seemed as if they were all covered with a layer of something dark, like rust.

With my finger, I pressed a mocha-brown lump, surrounded

by foam, which spread into a large stain on the curved wall. Pontanus' daughter touched its uneven, leathery surface and screamed. Mrs Raa came up to me and scratched the lump with her nail. She smelled the crumbs and said: 'I know this. It is Serpula lacrymans, the weeping fungus.'

True enough, we were wrong in supposing that no one lived in the house any more. Serpula lacrymans lived there. The name of the weeping fungus should have been written on the name-plate and in the deeds. Serpula lacrymans was now the master of the Tabernacle; it was the guardian spirit of the place.

We examined the Tabernacle from the crypt to the upper floor. The fungus's sabotage had, it seemed, begun in the cellar, but from there it had climbed by various different routes into the Pantheon and all the living rooms.

How can I describe Serpula lacrymans? It is not encountered in what is known as nature, only where people live. It is the most resourceful of creatures, for it feeds itself: it can not only steal, but also make, water. The weeping fungus drips cold tears, and the wood to which it clings, which it eats with its rust-rough, furrowed tongue, darkens, becomes fragile and crumbles into dust. It both grows inside the wood and spreads, in thick, labyrinthine tendons, along the wood's surface. With the effortlessness of an acrobat, it hurls its formlessness a metre or two across stone, concrete and glass to reach untouched, healthy wood.

And now, here in the Tabernacle, Serpula lacrymans had covered the walls and floors of the house around it with a furrowed, white-edged, dripping coverlet, and had also licked the ceilings with its greedy tongue. It seemed to me as if it had, here, also learned to eat stone...

All the visible surfaces were darkened, spotted with stains of mould and already partially rotted. Everywhere, paint was peeling or coming away in sheets, as though it had rained inside. This had been achieved by the incessant weeping of Serpula lacrymans.

I do not know, and neither did Mrs Raa or Latona, daughter of Pontanus, whether the Tabernacle had been abandoned on account of the fungus or whether it had conquered the house only after all the other inhabitants had left. Perhaps the Tabernacle had fallen ill because the Gold-Washers had abandoned it. Or perhaps the Gold-Washers had infected it with their own sickness...

It was certainly sad in the Pantheon, to look at the work of the hand of the Executioner, the Ziz bird, which the fungus was choking, and the eight-armed woman. For Serpula lacrymans had still more arms, whose sinewy branches embraced the smooth waist of the wooden girl. But the destruction looked worst upstairs, in the Kinswoman's former room.

Once that room had seemed to me more beautiful than any other home I knew. I had admired its lightness, its wall-paintings and its finely patinated parquet, its intarsia writing-desk, the tile stove and the royal blue carpet into which was woven the tree of life.

The writing-desk and the chest of drawers were now unpolished and blackened, the carpet dripping with water. How sad! The polished looking-glass, too, whose engraved frames were of the finest craftsmanship, the mirror, which had shown me my former face, had become dark and dull. One of the room's windows was gone, now that the perspective of the looking-glass was broken. Where, formerly, a way had opened to another, equally beautiful, world, the dirty map of an unknown continent had now appeared.

The room was now in harmony with the view that opened up to the west: there the refuse heaps of the Golden Reed welled up, a Hades of deceased objects.

Latona opened the door of the bookcase. I saw that Serpula lacrymans had climbed up the side of the bookcase and that its damp embrace had already vanquished many works. I remembered leafing through those same books, but now they were so badly eaten away that I could distinguish their names only with difficulty: *The Ancient World, The Tiger-Cat, Notebook, The Secret of the Cathedrals.*

We turned our gaze to the other corner.

A porcelain jug and cups were on the table, a samovar, a pile of neatly folded napkins whose corners were embroidered with violets. Once, these objects had reflected cleanliness, beauty and humanity into the room. But the weeping fungus had not passed even them by; no. Its lewd protruberances had grasped the table and its elastic, branching projections fringed even this little vision of happiness.

Serpula lacrymans crept under the plates, it hung in scrolls from the lip of the jug, the napkins had dulcified into rags at its touch, and the table-cloth, on which some sweet soul – probably the Glass-Girl – had embroidered ox-eye daisies, hung mouldily, full of holes.

'Let us take that crockery away from here,' said Mrs Raa.

But we did not want to touch it. Although Serpula lacrymans could not, of course, eat copper or porcelain, its touch seemed irrevocably to have destroyed even those beautiful objects.

I looked at them and thought: is this the end? I had never expected that the end could be like this, so damp and quiet.

We visited the other rooms, too. Most of them were empty, unlike the Kinswoman's room. In one, nevertheless, a terrarium had been left, which I had liked to look at when one of the Gold-Washers had kept book-lice there. Now it contained only stones and dust: the landscape itself, with its miniature pools, hillocks and copses had disappeared forever. When I pressed my forehead to the glass – how cold it was! – I thought I saw among the stones a single, yellowed wing, a few dry pieces of skin. That was all that was left of the book-lice.

We opened another door.

'Wasn't this my father's room?' asked Latona, the daughter of Pontanus.

Yes, this was Pontanus's chamber. My nose still sensed a

fine trace of sulphur, although the instruments and crucibles were now gone.

But not all of them. There was a small test-tube in a stand on the dusty shelf, which the scrolls of the weeping fungus were already reaching for.

I took it in my hand and turned it over. Why! Was it not familiar? Had I not held the same tube in my fingers before? There was no label on the tube, but I imagined that I recognised it. I opened the cork and sniffed. Inside was a dark, thick liquid. It did not smell of anything and it did not look like anything, but I believed that it had once held an example of the best results of Pontanus's work: a liquid that contained all the colours, the Peacock's Tail.

Before, when I had shaken it, it had been as if I had been able to see tiny flashes – a little red, some green. But now: nothing. And in this room, too, flowered the slimy frills of Serpula lacrymans.

Sad! So sad. As if one were looking at a familiar person whom illness had made almost unrecognisable...

'I'm cold,' said Mrs Raa. 'This is like a burial vault.'

'For God's sake, let us get out of here,' said Latona, the daughter of Pontanus. 'I feel as if that fungus had infected me, too. As if I had its spores in my throat.'

There was an edge of hysteria in her voice which did not please us. But she was right: we had seen enough. We needed to be under the clear sky.

That is how we became acquainted with Serpula lacrymans, the weeping fungus. And we realised that it is impossible to banish it if it has gained even an inch. But it itself drives all mortals into exile, both owners and tenants. For none of us would consent to live as a room-mate of Serpula lacrymans, moistened all over by its incessantly falling tears.

At the grave of the tuatara

Who would place a flower on the grave of the tuatara, that little monster? Who would feel longing or regret? Is it not, rather, a relief to know that one will never again have to look into its cold, round, skull-eye, which reflected the movements of the heavens so accurately, but in whose convex distorting mirror one saw one's own form bowing, out of proportion and ridiculously large-headed?

But when they arrived at that insignificant mound of earth, surrounded by stones that the children had placed in a circle so that, in its solitude, it recalled the graves of the Etruscans, they saw Babel there. Mr Babel, in other words, he who was also sometimes known by the name Mr Good-as-Gold.

He was crouching on the low stone like a frog, his face damp and contorted. He had not brought the tuatara flowers, either, although there were flowers to be seen there: a field of scabious, whose reddish, ball-like flowers nodded at the heads of their long stalks both inside the stone circle and outside it.

As always when they saw Babel, they were embarrassed, because they did not know what language they should speak to him; but, as was his custom, he released them from their difficulty by bursting into speech himself – at first, it was true, interruptedly, for deep sobs tore his chest.

Oh, had they not already had their share of weeping inside the rotting rooms of the Tabernacle... But these tears were of a different kind; they were fresh and yet warm.

And soon Babel's stream of speech was pattering as plentifully and naturally as real spring rain, and they could not understand his words any better than before. But they could hear that he was speaking sincerely and directly and of everything that was in his heart.

When he clasped their hands, one by one, and pressed them, looking into their faces with shining eyes, they began to comfort him like a child who has fallen over, and at the same time themselves and each other, as if the deceased were their dear and only friend or their own little one, as if he had only just been laid to rest and they were all part of a great funeral procession.

Were they hoping, at the grave of the tuatara, that when their turn came there would be someone whose words – if he were to remember them – would hold as living an echo as Babel's double Dutch?

But scarcely even one of them thought that the sorrow Babel expressed so freely concerned only the reptile's death. They could not know whether Babel was grieving more for the lost age of the Gold-Washers and the ruination of the Tabernacle or some private sorrow of which they knew nothing.

Or was he lamenting that apparently no fate had been prepared for them other than the one that small, scaly creature had already met, with its tail and its three eyes and its blood-spattering, wrinkled eyelids...

A light hand

Babel had squeezed my hand, too. When I withdrew my hand from his, I happened to look at my own. I raised it quite close to my eyes, and saw it, clearer than clear.

I turned it around in astonishment: How dry and white it had become. How full it was of criss-crossing, furrowed pathways!

I knew it already: they did not lead anywhere. I had traversed them all back and forth, back and forth, wearing them always deeper.

And there was scarcely anything more to be seen than the paths; there were so many of them, and they completely covered the continent formed by the back of my hand.

I made my hand into a fist, and a chain of mountains rose before my eyes: the lumpy bones of my knuckles. I saw the veins, which also rose as high, blue ridges. I spread my fingers in the air: and there was a trembling fan through which flew the wind of the mound.

It was a light, light hand, but it had become heavier and heavier to lift. That was because of the weight of memories, actions that originated here, but most of all those which it had never carried out. Just as the weeping fungus ate wood, memories ate human flesh, both good memories and bad ones.

They flowed with the increasingly sluggish circulation of the blood. They became the vital juice of humanity, its sap.

The more memories, the less blood. But they were not capable of nourishing people; they could nourish only their own independence.

Yes, I think that when a person dies, his memories go their own way: they fly in flocks of images and dreams, as a flight of birds leaving an impoverished nest. They float everywhere, let he who wishes grasp them; they no longer have a master, a homeland.

Babel and Mrs Raa and Latona, the daughter of Pontanus, were walking along, their heads close together, bent over, in the shadow cast by the waste heap.

How steep the sides of the heap had become, how its peaks grazed the clouds, like Aconcaqua, like Macchu Picchu.

Their triple shadow proceeded slowly along the sand road, past the fungus-eaten Tabernacle and the blackened framework of the pavilion. The pine-tree was green above them.

'Wait!'

I ran after them, limping with my left foot. Above the pine, very high, white slivers of wind had appeared, the first omens of approaching bad weather. The wind was already moving the swing that had once, long ago, been fixed to the lower branches of the pine, and on which the Child of the Tabernacle had once swung. It moved in wider and wider arcs. A thunderstorm would fly over the Tabernacle, perhaps quite soon. There had been more and more of them in recent times, and it was said that they presaged a fundamental change in the climate. It was time to return to the City of the Golden Road.

I listened as I stumbled forward. Was there the echo of a proud voice: 'Lived, but not gone, for it *has been* lived'?

Nothing like it was to be heard. But it was quiet, so deserted all around the grass-covered courtyard of the Tabernacle that behind the rising wind one could well have distinguished the merest whisper of one's own heart.

Like the wooden statue of the Tabernacle, and just as stiff, I felt the slimy touch of Serpula lacrymans.

But at that moment Babel stood still and gestured to me. I saw his mouth move, but he was already so far away that I could hear nothing. And even if I had heard, I would hardly have understood.

Suddenly something screeched in the opposite direction, not very close by. Was that what Babel had meant? It came from the abandoned building, from inside the darkening rooms of the Tabernacle.

And I knew that sound. It was the bowed harp which one of the Gold-Washers had scraped long ago. Just a couple of mischievous scrapes of the bow, which one could have confused with the wind that wound round the wings of the Tabernacle. But I had listened to the bowed harp so often with the Gold-Washers, during long evenings in the Tabernacle, that I remembered, that I knew, that I did not doubt for a second.

We were nearing the Tabernacle once more. And the bowed harp chirruped like a flock of memories.

The secret of famine-bread

Wheat-bread and famine-bread

We had been invited to the Tabernacle for dinner, to the Gold-Washers', I and Mrs Raa and Latona, the daughter of Pontanus, and the Customs Officer, who dissects bodies for a living.

Everyone expected something more excellent than usual: new and exotic foods, surprises and entertainments, nuances of enjoyment not only for the palate but also for the eyes and the ears. For the Gold-Washers knew how to arrange festivals, whether there was any reason for them or not.

For my part, I can openly confess my astonishment when we arrived in the dining-room and saw that it had not been decorated in any way. The table had been set, it was true, but there was no cloth, let alone flowers or candles. Plain white plates and ordinary water-glasses had been set directly on the scratched, wooden surface of the table.

We sat down. For some reason – or perhaps merely because of the frugal surroundings – everyone changed, became melancholy and silent. Even Mr Babel, who, as we had entered the room, had managed to clap his hands together and say melodiously, 'Chanta!' – even he was silent, as was the Gold-Washer whose monologue had already lasted for many years. Only the Kinswoman guffawed to herself and seemed satisfied with her surroundings.

One of the Gold-Washers circled the table and poured water, plain water into each glass from a carafe. A second Gold-Washer had taken up a position next to the wall, a stringed instrument in his lap. From time to time the instrument let out a tired squeak.

A third Gold-Washer clapped his hands and suggested we raise our glasses. Our glasses? When all we had to drink was water...

What should we drink to?

'First,' said the first Gold-Washer, 'I suggest we drink to poverty.'

'Poverty? Really?' asked Mrs Raa.

But Babel was ready at once. He leaped up and nodded to everyone, his water-glass outstretched. Very well, we drank to poverty, why not drink to poverty.

'Second,' said the first Gold-Washer, 'I suggest we drink to solitude.'

'We should clink just one glass to that,' said Pontanus. 'That would be the true sound of solitude.'

But we clinked glasses to solitude with everyone, with every glass.

'Third,' said the first Gold-Washer, 'I suggest we drink to thirst.'

'I suppose we should clink empty glasses,' said Pontanus, the father of Latona. 'That is the sound of thirst.'

But there was still a drop of water in our glasses, and so we drank, too, to thirst, and at the same time drained our glasses.

Then the third Gold-Washer came in, bearing aloft a great tray. We did not see what was on the tray until he set it on the table before us.

On it was some kind of cake, still steaming, rather soggy, of indeterminate shape. It recalled a piece of peat or a cow-pat, and its smell, too, was that of earth in autumn.

'What is it?' asked Mrs Raa.

'It is famine-bread,' said the first Gold-Washer.

'Famine-bread,' said Mrs Raa. 'Yes, of course, what else.'

'What is the recipe for famine-bread?' I asked.

'Spread straw on the threshing-floor,' said the Gold-Washer. 'Then take a stamper and thrash with it until the ears come away from the stems. Grind to flour with the straw, husks and chaff. Add water and yeast, if you have it. Mix into a dough and pat into loaves. That is the secret of famine-bread.'

Silence descended on the company at table, the long silence of a famine-year. There was a glimmer over the cake as the third Gold-Washer raised a silver cake-trowel. It was the only costly thing at this dining table.

'Well,' he said commandingly, 'who will go first?'

Mrs Raa offered her plate hesitantly, and then I and Mr Babel, a real epicure, and Pontanus and the Kinswoman and everyone else; no one refused.

The famine-bread had just been taken from the oven and was still so hot that we rolled it on our tongues for a long time. It was rough. It was bitter. It was hard to chew, and still harder to swallow, it seemed to be full of awns that stuck in the throat, so that the second Gold-Washer had constantly to fill our glasses.

But as soon as the first sensation of the famine-bread had reached some distant shore within me, I began to see with the taste-buds of my tongue. I saw the serrated edge of the wildwoods, and grey, shingle-covered cabins, low cowsheds, storehouses, saunas, barns and stables. I saw in and I saw out. A thin nag dragged its load up a sandy slope, the shadows of cockroaches flitted through smoke-darkened rooms. A mongrel growled. An old man went into the forest, an axe on his shoulder.

My land and my people! Who existed no longer. I stood at the edge of a field of stubble, a flock of crows flew over the dazzling surface of the lake. Women were binding sheaves; in a basket at the edge of the field a baby was crying with hunger.

'A very singular taste,' said the Customs Officer.

He coughed and drank. On Mr Babel's now pallid face there was real suffering, but his teeth went on grinding away.

'Say it straight: it's horrible,' said the first Gold-Washer. 'You don't like it, and I don't like it, either. It's the taste of pine-bark, which we have long since forgotten. It is the taste of hunger. Now we are tasting it, so that we may remember.

Accustom yourselves to its aromas. Be tolerant toward it. Perhaps there will yet come a time when we shall rejoice even in crumbs of famine-bread – if we do not fight over them. Perhaps there will come a time when it is our daily bread, for which we have to beg. Play!'

And the stringed instrument, which had fallen silent for a moment, began to whine once more. What a dinner party! We picked the chaff from the corners of our mouths and drank more water. For many, eating became overwhelmingly difficult after the first mouthful, and knives and forks remained on the plate beside almost untouched pieces of famine-bread.

The stringed instrument did not cease screeching in my ear. The Gold-Washer who strummed it hummed over my head:

As you bite into the loaf
The illusion's shed
What you thought was wheat
Is pine-bark, famine-bread.

Only the jaws of Mr Babel and the first Gold-Washer continued to move until their plates were empty.

'Just a little practice,' the first Gold-Washer encouraged the dinner-guests. 'If you just chew carefully, it's not too bad, we mustn't be discouraged. We'll get used to it.'

But he pushed his plate away and raised his glass.

'Relax,' he shouted earsplittingly, and clapped his hands once more.

The door opened again. Through it came more Gold-Washers, carrying trays, their arms held out before them. They were laden with bottles of wine and Burgundy ham, roast pheasant and Caribbean heart stew and, to crown it all: a lemon syllabub.

The stringed instrument was put away, but a guitar and a bamboo flute began to play, a glass harmonica tinkled and a triangle, bright as silver. Chrysanthemums and thin-stemmed glasses appeared on the table, and candles were lit in every room and in the garden, where it was already night.

The plates of famine-bread were speeded away. At once the atmosphere lightened. We ate and laughed. The heavy weight of the famine-bread had disappeared from the table, and the reek of poverty from our nostrils.

This was, once more, the Tabernacle we knew.

The wafer

Later, as we walked in the garden lit by lamps and candles, animated by the wine, we saw under a tree the tuatara, the strange pet of the Gold-Washers. It was eating. The remains of our first course had been set before it, the bitter famine food of our forefathers.

Would it be fit even for the tuatara? It looked as if it was, and more: the tuatara smacked its lips and sneezed as it ate, but it ate with devotion, entirely absorbed in its task. The tuatara was not fastidious.

Only as I watched it did I notice that autumn had come to the garden. How quickly it had come! While we had been fretfully chewing our famine-bread...

Everything, everything withered, and the colours of autumn spread over the earth in a golden cloak. Blazing with its autumn, a tree shed its leaves on to the slippery back of the tuatara. They fell and covered its third eye, poured over the corrugated ridge on its back, blew in endless showers over its nocturnal meal, over the Tabernacle's bitter bread of life, the wafer we had rejected.

Home-sickness

The City of the Golden Reed

This is the city, the rowdy village, that the angel measured with his golden reed. It is twelve thousand furlongs in length and breadth and height.

The smoke of the city spreads far. Its light-pollution hides the stars and the night from view. Stone everywhere, flesh everywhere. Jasper and sardonyx. Concrete and glass. And sometimes flesh is colder than stone, and sometimes stone is as warm and seductive as human skin.

Here is a drink that never ceases to ferment, a fortified extract. So dense with events that the gaze must be like a knife in order to clear its own path to this point.

Who can predict the movements and future of so complex an organism? In its incompleteness it is as alluring as a glimpse of a stranger. He steps out of nothing and points toward the window of a florist's shop just as the tram turns down another street, so that his gesture is never completed.

But I turn my eyes in time, and behind the panes of glass, from the other side of the reflections and their reflections, blaze the cooling flames of gerberas, irises and narcissi.

Eyes cruise up and down the streets, always two by two. Refractors. Pupils. Tunnels of lenses. Through them pass the lights of the city and through them, out of a night protected by the vitreous humour, out of a seeing invisibility, the whole city has streamed forth.

When their former owners disappear, the eyes seek new ones for themselves. And many of them have indeed disappeared! One no longer sees even officers here, their greatcoats flapping in the constant wind, or weavers or swordsmiths or Mrs Bock, who used to ride in the magistrate's carriage in her frock decorated with rosettes.

The Cossack general Krasnasyol has been murdered. No

one remembers the shame of Lindström, the street tobacconist, any longer: that he was whipped for stealing a horse where Ore Street now ends. The potato-sellers no longer shout from their roughly made carts whose rattling wheels echoed to the end of the street. The eyes have changed, now they sit well in the heads of tax accountants and demonstrators of new products and qualified restaurant-keepers and countless old women who consider death their particular privilege.

How busy they are in their rush to get from one place to another. How they tack through the stream of shadows, the cross-swell of intersecting streets. How hurried I am, how I rush.

Beneath the giant spectacles of the optician and the barber's golden platter, past the sun of the solarium and the booming bowling hall and the aquarium shop in whose window a tarantula is eating flies, through the park, where the monuments to those who have died of the plague are being cleaned.

Many wish to be far away from here; I do not. I listen to the sounds of the city as if the angel were blowing them into the air with his golden reed.

For this, too, and precisely this, is the City of the Golden Reed. It has been measured by an angel, and it is, in length and breadth and height, twelve thousand furlongs.

Ding and dong

But can one place one's trust in it, the City of the Golden Reed? For every place here wanders like a nomad; dust rises.

Scarcely have chains of mountains risen – variscan, appalachian, alpine – than they immediately begin to level. Continental plates shudder, seas dry into jungles of salt and swell once more. Like facial expressions and human ages, the landscapes of the earth's surface change.

The city is a real but molten substance, like ectoplasm, which never solidifies. The thoughts of the crowd, people's actions, hammer at the city, and its shape changes; its form is never completed.

Some people said Mrs Raa was away for two years, or three; others that she was not seen in the city for almost a decade; but most said nothing, for her name was unknown to them.

Bells! First of all, that little tinkling of bells... It danced mischievously into her ears from the fresh streets from which the snow had melted like the memory of a shared dream. It mixed with the slapping of the soft points of shoes against stone and recalled something long-forgotten to her mind. But Mrs Raa had never before seen such peculiar shoes.

First of all, they were very brightly coloured, garish really: crimson red, electric blue, green and violet, saffron- and sun-yellow. Sometimes one even saw shoes crowded with all the five hundred thousand colours of the spectrum, in spots, torrents of lines, whirls and spirals. If one looked at them for too long, one soon had to blink.

But the most extraordinary thing, for Mrs Raa, was not the colours, but the shape and size of the shoes. For during her absence they had grown so exaggeratedly long at their points that one would have thought they would make walking difficult. And indeed they did, for the longest points were often fastened with cords to the walker's knees. Others had various objects fastened to them as amulets, or those little bells that tinkled on every square and pavement.

When Mrs Raa raised her eyes, she saw brightly coloured leggings or tight trousers that looked like leggings, but which were as gaudy as the shoes, but one leg was often of a different colour from the other.

And whatever detail her eyes fastened upon in the dress of passers-by, everywhere she found the same spirit of excess, the same pomp approaching effrontery, which expressed itself in immoderately large buttons, sleeves puffed up with starch, and collars that fell across the chest. Their folds were rustled by the gusts of wind that were always rushing through the city.

The clothes of new citizens mixed distant periods and foreign traditions with what they believed to be hitherto unprecedented.

Mrs Raa came to me in a passion and said:

'But they wear old lace headdresses and saris, caftans and monks' cowls. Are they Buryats? Fellahs? Franciscans? This is not the city I knew.'

'What did you expect?'

I laughed and swung my legs so that the little bell at the tip of my shoe tinkled brightly. 'Don't they use shoe-bells down there in the south, then?'

But Mrs Raa was right: the city had changed. Was that a bad thing? Wasn't it just as it should be. The tinkling was cheerful, it pleased my ear and it pleased Mrs Raa's ear; but she was anxious.

'It's not just the clothes,' she said. 'It's the air, people and people's conversation. There's too much of everything.'

Did I not understand what she was keeping faith with, what she was remembering in speaking in such a way. Her former city! Our city! When Mrs Raa called it up from her memory, it rose before her from the bath of decades as modest and austere as long ago. It was cool, sure enough, but at the same time clean and modest. It was raining, and she was so short that she could see the street paving stones quite close; they gleamed wetly, they refracted the light like precious stones, like jasper, like sardonyx. And there were no hues of such fineness, of such richness, in the citizens' new clothes.

Women and men (both dong and ding)
summer autumn winter spring
reaped their sowing and went their came
sun moon stars rain

All around her little fountains were born and died as drops shattered on the stones and the wind spread their freshness over the square.

The war had ended; in the noonday park a dove was pecking at the sand and making do with what it found. A window opened, sparkling, and their mother's voice tumbled over them like home, where the running footstep rested, where satisfaction and poverty resided.

Not even the patience of an archaeologist can return her former city to Mrs Raa. And what if it could? How sad, how strange would be the Mrs Raa who lived there...

The dark shadow of the pleasure palace…

The Gold-Washers had an idea. It was a simple, megalomanic idea. They thought it was possible to build a house in which life would be different and better than elsewhere. That on the crumbling surface of the earth it would be possible to found a stronghold, to set aside an area of quiet waters that norns and demons would avoid.

Perhaps many other homes, too, have been built in such a belief, but I learned to know only the Tabernacle.

It was not really a temple, and neither were the Gold-Washers, its inhabitants, any more pious than the other citizens. They merely had a pinch of faith and a lot of money – whose, never became clear to me.

When we saw it for the first time, Mrs Raa and I and Latona, the daughter of Pontanus, it made us laugh a little. It was a misty day and as we approached the Tabernacle it materialised rapidly, as if it had not been built of wood and concrete and glass, but of some much more fluid substance.

It was not in a place where any of us would have wished to build a house. The refuse dump of the City of the Golden Reed was too close. We sensed its stench, we saw its disintegrating heaps and the screaming flocks of gulls above it.

The Tabernacle, the pleasure palace of the Gold-Washers, was unlike any house we had ever seen before, although it contained parts and materials from many buildings that we knew only from pictures.

'What architect designed this?' asked Mrs Raa. 'Is he still at large?'

Although the Tabernacle was in the City of the Golden Reed, on its outer edge, it did not seem to have a home town. It was a lonely house, it was a house of great confusion.

'Porta Maggiore!' cried Latona.

'Not in the least, from this side it's St Peter's,' I said.

'No, no,' said Mrs Raa. 'Don't you remember? It's the spitting image of Hagia Sofia.'

'But that tower,' I said. 'That's the tower of the Admiralty.'

But I also noted the pointed arches of curved wood. They had been made by a Gothic spirit that had found itself in the wrong age. Where, then, did the crooked walls, the Tabernacle's asymmetry and its peculiar sense of imbalance come from? Its geometry provoked anxiety, the building moved and never really became fixed to the spot.

Before us was confusion, nobility and the power of hope, which was only increased by the scaffolding which had been left there.

There were also some columns, a loggia which proceeded like a solemn, expansive thought. But the curves of the roof dizzied the gaze; they were the Tabernacle's earthly wings.

'This sort of thing shouldn't be allowed,' said Mrs Raa. 'It really shouldn't.'

We went on standing there, in the gravel of the road, gazing around us, until Pontanus came and took us inside.

'This is the Pantheon,' he said.

We found ourselves among statues in a round, draughty vestibule. They had been placed in semicircular niches in the walls of the hall, but some of the spaces were still awaiting their inhabitants. They were monstrous or divine forms: a melancholy sphinx, a kalamakara, an archaeoptrix. I touched them, I stroked their surface with my finger and realised that they were all made of wood: aspen, spruce, pine.

'Who made those?' I asked.

'The Executioner,' said Pontanus. 'He lives here.'

There seemed to be a countless number of rooms in the Tabernacle, and not one of them resembled another. One of them was of bamboo and paper; its floor was covered in sisal matting. One was triangular, another semicircular, a third had walls but no roof, a fourth a roof but only two walls.

There were empty rooms which had no furniture, or only a mattress on the floor, and others that were furnished extravagantly, some ostentatiously, some elegantly. It seemed to me that these rooms were public spaces; I did not believe anyone lived in them. We also passed closed doors, but we did not meet any of the building's inhabitants.

'Would you like to see the most beautiful room in the Tabernacle?' Pontanus asked.

He took us to the upper floor, to the western gable of the building. There was a spacious, light-filled room which one could see in three directions, every way but north.

I had certainly never seen such a beautiful room, and neither had Mrs Raa or Latona, the daughter of Pontanus. It was beautiful in a classical, thoroughly bourgeois way.

And it was no ordinary room, either: it was a salon or drawing-room. On the wall were painted, with exceptional skill, columns, bunches of grapes and medallions and another door, whose handle I went to turn before I realised that it was painted.

I also saw a solemn canopied bed which was like a room within a room. On a curved walnut bureau stood a heavy candelabrum. The sunlight, which flooded in from all directions, was softened by white curtains and glowed in the polished mirrors behind the candlestick and in the roses, white and red. There were three vases of them before each window.

A glass-doored bookcase was of the same reddish walnut as the bureau.

Between the doors – the real door and the illusory door – was a small square piano. The floor was covered by a blue carpet edged with narrow, meandering patterns. In the centre of the carpet a tree spread its branches, carrying both flowers and fruit.

It was a beautiful and exquisite carpet, perfect for the floor of so rare a room.

'Who lives in this room? You?' I asked.

'Not me. This is the Kinswoman's room,' Pontanus answered. Across his face there flickered a somehow unpleasant expression, memory or thought which I did not have time to decipher.

'Who is she?'

'You will meet her soon enough,' said Pontanus.

He looked out of the window and I went to stand beside him. I should have remembered what to expect, but all the same I started a little. The view to the west, over the rose-vases, was like a defamation when one looked at it from the constant peace of the Kinswoman's room.

There rose apennines of waste, rotting refuse and abandoned piles of things, behind which the sun was just setting. It was strange and wrong that the substance of things lasted so much longer than human flesh, which withered and was forgotten like flowers.

'What luck!' said Pontanus, and leaned, looking dreamy, against the window-sill as if he were admiring the alpine glow.

'What luck are you talking about?' asked Mrs Raa.

'That we were able to build the Tabernacle just here,' he said.

'What kind of luck is that,' asked Latona, his daughter. 'Those junk heaps aren't beautiful, and what's more, they smell.'

'You don't understand,' Pontanus said. 'This refuse site will soon be full. Next year, or perhaps even before Christmas, it will be closed, and then they will begin to build a big park in its place. It will be levelled, soil will be brought here, lawns will be sown and flowers and trees planted. It will be a real sight – I have heard it will be the biggest park in the whole of the City of the Golden Reed.'

'Perhaps even a rose-garden,' I said.

'Oh, father, you'll believe anything,' said Latona, daughter of Pontanus, and Mrs Raa hummed:

For you have promised unto us
that even to the wilderness
will come a lovely spring . . .

But as we looked at those terrible cordilleras, we wanted, nevertheless, to believe, as Pontanus believed.

Nocturnal letters

Mrs Raa got a lot of mail; she received a letter almost every night.

The first, original letter, of which all the other nocturnal letters were the consequence, was written by her husband. On it was only her name, nothing else, for they lived, of course, at the same address then; there had been no need to drop the letter into a mail-box.

Mrs Raa saw the first letter on the kitchen table immediately after she had found her husband's body, still warm, in the car in the garage. The envelope was carefully sealed, and Mrs Raa was afraid of it.

When all the formalities had been attended to, Mrs Raa took the letter in her hand. She turned it over in her hands and then dropped it on the table as if it had burnt her. It was a day and a night before she was able to open it.

The envelope was empty. There was nothing in it, not even an unwritten sheet. It was just an envelope.

For a long time Mrs Raa looked for the piece of paper that her husband had intended to put in the envelope. He had always been absent-minded. But when Mrs Raa had emptied and gone through her dead husband's desk drawers, the piles of paper on his writing table, the book-case, the kitchen cupboards and all the waste-paper bins, she realised that there was no such piece of paper. The lightness of the letter was the same as the lightness of her own life, the clothes and the skin and the apartment that covered the desolation of her heart like dry shells.

After the funeral, Mrs Raa moved back to her home city. But mail came to the City of the Golden Reed, too, from the place where her spouse now was. Mrs Raa found a letter on the kitchen table of her new apartment almost every night.

Always her name was written on it in her husband's small handwriting. But Mrs Raa could not reply: she had no address.

In the second letter she read the words that she had most feared: IT WAS YOU.

When she opened the third letter, all the lights in her house were burning. But from inside the letter flowed darkness, which spread quickly from room to room. The lights dimmed, she could no longer see anything. She wanted to close the envelope, but could no longer find it. The night around her was not mere darkness, but a blindness that filled every corner.

The fourth letter contained a plan of their house. It resembled some kind of orientation map, or the treasure charts children make, for in one of the rooms of the apartment, in a corner of the hall, a cross had been drawn. She saw herself wander through the hall with the map in her hand and stand in the corner marked by the cross. There was nothing there but a pile of old newspapers awaiting the next collection of waste paper. The pile was alarmingly high and crooked, and it looked to her as if it must contain a newspaper for every day of her life.

From the fifth letter her husband rose, looking just the same as before, but of course he was much smaller, hardly the length of a pencil. Joy and peace, the vision of a new possibility, made Mrs Raa's heart dizzy.

Her husband began to grow, quickly, quickly, and soon he was the right size and Mrs Raa pressed him to her breast. But he continued to swell, at astonishing speed, and Mrs Raa's arms could no longer encircle him. They could not restrain such unbridled growth. Her husband's shoulders were already touching the walls, his head tore open the ceiling, but after that he began to vaporise. His solidity disappeared and he became summer mist, ether, the smoke of distant campfires.

When Mrs Raa opened the sixth letter, a light scent wafted

from it. Mrs Raa did not know what scent it was, that of a flower or a fruit or the scent of their former love, which had been lost long before her husband's death, or which she had imagined had been lost. Mrs Raa liked the scent; she did not want it to evaporate. But it evaporated even before she awoke.

Inside the seventh envelope was a piece of lined paper, as if torn from a school exercise book. On it was drawn various objects: a water-glass, an onion, a teaspoon, a chair. The drawings were rough and approximate, for her husband had never been able to draw, and the objects were simple, ordinary objects, of a kind that Mrs Raa had grown used to seeing and using every day.

She turned the piece of paper over in her hands and wondered whether it was a picture-riddle, a puzzle picture. But she could not think of a solution.

Mrs Raa kept the empty envelope in the drawer of her night-table. After dreaming, she sometimes opened the drawer and looked inside the envelope once more. Then she got up and went into the kitchen and let the water run. It was tomorrow and she drank a glass of water in the immeasurable light of the east window. But the chambers of her heart had turned into court chambers in which complex legal cases were heard.

When she sat down, the chair said a word, she stirred her coffee with a spoon and, in the dawn, her eyes were the eyes of an onion-peeler.

The ravens of Edom

In the rooms of the Tabernacle, in the pavilion, in the courtyards, there were to be seen, increasingly often, two already aged figures who moved with difficulty. If one asked the Gold-Washers their names, one heard only: the ravens of Edom.

Perhaps they were man and wife, perhaps they had once had a home in a small town far to the north. But that was a long time ago: when I met them, they no longer had a home, a town of their own. Who knows what had happened to them? Who was even interested? For their home town was so poor and insignificant, and so far away in the north.

No foreign power had conquered it, it had not been fought for from street to street, and no one had manned the barricades to defend it. What had happened had happened in silence.

The houses emptied and their doors and windows were barred. The school playground was deserted. Even in the heart of winter, not even the thinnest thread of smoke rose from a single chimney.

You grew silent, town, and your streets
remain empty: not a soul
will return, say why you were abandoned

They went away, to the south, in a forced emigration, their native town died: there is no eye to see it.

For not only people, animals and plants are mortal: places, too, can die. Places, too, can be mourned like dead people.

Now those who lived there were scattered like the tribe of Judah, like straws in the winds of the wilderness. Some fell in the interior, some on the coast, like this old couple. Each one of them carried with them their little town, pocket-sized.

Their old home was only an empty shell. The real town, built of people, had been wiped off the map and only wild animals lived there, thinned out by hunger and extinction.

What were those two doing in the Tabernacle, with the Gold-Washers, among people of a quite different race?

They were permitted to live in one of the rooms of the pleasure palace, and someone thought he knew: 'They have been adopted.'

They wandered through the Tabernacle like children lost in the forest, like Hansel and Gretel. One mumbled incessantly to herself, the other stared persistently at the floor as if looking for a trail of crumbs of bread that would guide him back home.

The Customs Officer, he who dissected bodies for a living, brought them sparkling glasses and said: 'You are from such-and-such a place, aren't you?'

And they looked at him, reviving: 'Have you ever been there?'

'Once,' said the Customs Officer, and tried to think of something kind to say about that miserable, cold town.

'It was a beautiful spot,' he seemed to remember at last. 'Yes... so peaceful.'

'Isn't that right?' said one of them, grateful for his words. And the other: 'The streams of Edom shall be turned into pitch, and her soil into brimstone; her land shall become burning pitch.'

'What did you say?' asked the Customs Officer.

'Night and day it shall not be quenched; its smoke shall go up for ever. From generation to generation it shall lie waste; none shall pass through it for ever and ever. But the hawk and the porcupine shall possess it, the owl and the raven shall dwell in it. He shall stretch the line of confusion over it, and the plummet of chaos over its nobles.'

The Customs Officer looked for a means of escape, but the homeless man's voice was already becoming more uncertain; it began to fragment and grow dim. The ravens of Edom left the Customs Officer and continued their progress past groups of talking people and self-absorbed couples.

'Is that where they come from?' someone asked, and was answered: 'Yes, there.'

But no one saw the cloud the ravens of Edom had spun about them. It was their aura, the extension of their personality, and surrounded by it they wandered through the Tabernacle as they wandered anywhere else that was not Edom. It was the dense cloud of home-sickness, the only faithful companion in the trials of exile, on the road to Hooronaim.

Just as the soil has its own irradiance and the sky its own, so their lives, too, were radiant; evenly and incessantly, their cloud radiated a grief which was hardly likely to reach its half-life.

But the cloud shed light, it threw out a beam of light, and raised their past up as if on a platform. And in the limelight every detail, every task, every object under the lost sky of Edom took on a new significance, and its colours were cleansed like the patterns on stones in shore-water.

And their ancient days had, indeed, been days of happiness. How exile broadened them, and what a rainbow it hurled across the hinterland town that jutted out on the shore of its unacidified lake with its modest apartment blocks, sawmills and cut-price supermarkets and constantly beflagged petrol stations.

The illumination of their home-sickness was shadowless, all-embracing. Their former life was superabundantly rich in the light of that cloud.

If the ravens of Edom could once return, if they could see their little Edom again as it was, what would happen to them? Would they return to their former tasks, accustoming themselves once more to the everyday life of Edom, and growing tired of it? How soon would they forget that which had been longer and broader and higher than anything else in their lives: their own home-sickness and its clear-sightedness?

The glow of the Gold-Washers

The tail of the peacock

'What is this?'

'Just water,' Pontanus said.

'And this?'

'Mercury.'

'And this?'

'Lead.'

'And that?'

'Tin.'

Scales and weights. Living fire and the green eye of the monitor. Crucibles and measuring glasses of all sizes, on their sides the images of the flames. Coloured fluids, bubbling. Powders. Smells and evaporators.

But through them I saw, day by day, Pontanus's precise hands, the hands of an illusionist, weighing and sprinkling, shaking and mixing, measuring and arranging.

I fingered Pontanus's tools. I turned in this direction and that in his cramped room in the Tabernacle building and could not avoid breathing in sulphur fumes. I asked whatever came into my head and he answered, patiently, but lost in his own thoughts.

Pontanus believes everything is alive: the air and the earth, fire and water, but also the rock on which the city is founded, minerals and metals, every substance we encounter, we covet or evade – dead people, too, and that which cannot be seen and of which we know nothing.

Oh Pontanus, poor Pontanus. His words are the after-images of centuries that have been trodden to dust. What is the water of which he speaks, the dry water that does not wet the hand? Where is the gentle fire that does not smoke? A continuous, unchanging fire, like a stone? A fire like liquid, a fire that transfixes, a single entity?

Not to mention all the colours! He sprays me with his saliva as he tells me of a black that is the source of white, and of a white in which red is hidden.

'It is forty-two days before the black phase begins,' he says. 'If I don't make any mistakes. Then ninety days to the white phase, and to the red five months, at least.'

'Is that when it is ready?'

'It is,' he says, and in his voice there is not the slightest quiver of doubt.

But I know that he has been engaged in the same work for at least a year, a year and a half, and there is no sign yet of the black phase. But Pontanus is not one to be downhearted. Not Pontanus. Night falls, and he does not tire, but becomes more alert, his finger rises and he raves about a quintessence that is the fifth element, and elixirs and antimonies, a king and queen, an eagle and a frog, and the Green Lion.

Pontanus is not satisfied with his role as a dependent variable, as an eyewitness. He wishes to be more than witness and a victim: he who does, changes and exchanges, rejects and chooses. He wishes himself to be God, and is that strange? That is what everyone wants! Everyone who is a real, living person…

But many acquaintances shake their heads. They ask: 'Is he a lunatic, a madman?'

And I confess that I, too, can laugh at him, but not here, not as I see his rough face sweating behind the clouds of steam. Not as I see in his eyes the same golden glow that he tries to entice from his brews.

His gravity, his stone-quiet forehead cannot but draw me to him. Even when his mouth speaks with a spray of spittle, his forehead keeps silence, steep and white.

What, then, does he want? To transform the common into the rare, the rough into the sublime, the valueless into the immeasurably precious. He, a slight and short man, believes he can, like the womb of the earth itself, ripen and breed; like the ocean, enrich and crystallise.

And he claims that everything comes from one, which is two. That from two, one will come once more, through the Great Work.

It is no use arguing with Pontanus that he is a century, or even a thousand years, too late. Did not the world of which he speaks – the world of crystal spheres – long ago break into fragments, with its unicorns and chimeras? It was a beautiful but cruel world, yet not as merciless as this new one.

For now we find ourselves together in a world more desolate from year to year, of which both animals and gods are taking their leave.

'Tell me, Pontanus, would you like to have it back? Would you like to exchange the red shift and neutrinos for perdition and the brilliance of crystal spheres, nucleotides and polymers for makaras and basilisks, waves, particles and radiation for God's plan, absolute, mathematical, real time?'

Laugh at Pontanus, mock him. He will stand firm, he will tell you that although much has been found, much has also been lost, that although much has been learned, much has been forgotten.

I listen to him with pleasure, but at the same time in sorrow. I look from the darkness of my own melancholy at how he boils and mixes, sublimates and refines his multi-coloured distillates in his little room, which he has dedicated as the chamber of the Great Work. I take a measuring glass in my hand and ask, 'What's in here?'

'Salt,' he answers.

'And here?'

'Mercury.'

'And here, ugh?'

'Sulphur.'

Often he answers readily, but often he breaks off and waves his hands: no point, in vain. But if I am too eager to say, 'I understand,' he becomes angry and makes it clear that it is not as simple as all that. Do I imagine that I can understand in the twinkling of an eye something that it has taken him years, or even decades, to comprehend?

There are matters about which he keeps a decided silence. He says they are things about which he cannot yet speak: his lips are sealed. When I ask what, in the end, is the final aim of his efforts, I do not receive a straight answer. All in all, he speaks confusingly and badly; however attentively I listen to him, I cannot understand the connections, and I begin to grow anxious, even fearful.

He does indeed have the hands of an illusionist, but much less to show than a master of trickery. I bid him farewell, return to the streets of the Golden Reed; there is a damp wind, the vapours of his room soon disperse from my hair.

But not a week has gone by before I am sitting in his laboratory once more, turning over in my hands a crucible that holds a foaming green liquid, or another, which he calls the Tail of the Peacock. It is supposed to contain all the colours.

'There is a rainbow here,' says Pontanus.

To me, the contents of the bottle are cloudy and obscure, like wine sediment. It smells bad. But if one shakes the bottle hard, there is a flash of red, a flicker of green stripe. It does not look like anything at all, just like a patch of petrol glistening on the surface of a puddle.

Why on earth have I come here again? Because, even if I do not understand what he says, although, like the others, I feel sorry for him and fear that he is wasting his time, I believe I secretly understand what he wants. I would not dare confess it even to him: a furrow of doubt appears again and again at the corner of my mouth and often I raise my eyebrows. But is not what most people do for a living in this city even more insignificant, more useless, than what Pontanus does?

That is why I never tell him what the others say: that his work is hopeless and pointless. For if I were to say it to him, should I not also have to say it to myself?

For in what essential sense do my own endeavours differ

from Pontanus's work? Do I, too, in my own room, life, body, not distil and vaporise, sublimate and decoct and mix the raw substances that I have been given, the days of my life, this time, this flesh, that it might be more than decomposing substance? That the best might be distilled and sublimated from it, that it might endure as gold endures? Do I, too, not wish to fashion it into something other than what it is, something other than what it appears to be? Is this not my real employment?

Do I not hope that joy might burst forth from these worthless, snuffed-out days, as colourful as the floating tail of the peacock – that from them, through the chemistry of my own longing, the wonderful star of antimony, the regulus star, pure as crystal, might once again condense?

The pans

What pans they had! A shake! and the nuggets of gold separated from the gravel of days. They were few, and the gravel and clay and sludge and mud were plentiful. But there were some! There were! No one can make me say there were not.

I am not of the same feather as they, but something about the Gold-Washers attracted me. There was in them a burning focus, as in all monomaniacs, the blessed focus of madness, which warmed my melancholy, cold-blooded lizard-nature. Warmed it for a time, until it cooled, and I crawled on my way, seeking new sources of heat...

Their names, like their individuality, were embedded in the great clan of Gold-Washers, its family similarity, its continuity, its endless hospitality, which fused together their individual dreams.

If I wish, I can certainly remember him who sat in front of a microscope or stared at the terrarium all night long. What, really, was he examining so fixedly? In a box beside him were small insects, only two millimetres long. They were dead creatures, which he dissected and prepared. All of them belonged to one and the same family of lice, Copeognatha, to its sub-sect, Atropos pulsatorium.

Once I stopped to look as he did his work. When I had seen enough, I asked: 'What do you want with those crawling things? What makes them so interesting that, from one day to the next, you enjoy their company so much that you will soon begin to look more like them than like people?'

The Gold-Washer said: 'If only you knew how tired I am of faces and expressions and words. This little book-louse is marvellous. It does not bother us, or ever say a single word. Its world lies next to ours and we know nothing of it, but from the inside, from the book-louse's point of view, it is as boundless as the world of human beings. Bigger, even, for it is smaller than ourselves. I shall show it to people; I am writing a report whose title will be *The Past, Meaning and Destiny of the Book-Louse.*'

This Gold-Washer also had a couple of bees' nests at the end of the garden, beside the coppice behind which the piles of waste undulated.

'To produce a pound of honey,' the Gold-Washer once said, 'a bee must visit seven million five hundred thousand flowers.'

That truly amazed me. I could not understand how the Gold-Washer's bumblebees could find, in such a landscape, seven million five hundred thousand flowers.

But I remembered Pontanus's dream.

Another Gold-Washer joined us. He wore a tall, flat-topped hat on his head, a kind of top-hat, except that it was not black. On the contrary, it was of innumerable colours, sparkling, brilliant, almost self-luminous colours. His hat was as garishly multi-coloured as the citizens' new shoes. It was a provocative, vulgar hat that called many things into question.

But it was not by any means the Gold-Washer's only headdress. Sometimes he dressed in a tricorn hat, sometimes a turban or a red fez, a skullcap or a ridiculous drainpipe cap.

When, after we first became acquainted, I tried to recall this Gold-Washer's face, I saw before me only a furiously rotating cylinder, glittering with colours.

And I never really remembered his face, even later, but I did recall his voice, and he had many voices – for he both sang and played. He played the bullroarer and the comb and the split drum and a home-made glass harmonica – anything from which he could coax a sound.

The third Gold-Washer was the Executioner. It was he who had made, with chisel and axe and plane, the strange wooden statues of the Tabernacle, and had also made many kinds of furniture for the building. He did not speak at all, and did not like his work to be interrupted. Sombre and bearded, he hewed, whittled, planed and polished.

If anyone asked him, as he busied himself at his block of wood as if it were an executioner's block, 'What are you making?' he growled, 'A statue,' and continued working without pause.

But there was also a Gold-Washer who did nothing. It seemed to me, in fact, that he had never done anything at all. He did not dissect book-lice or sing or play, he did not make statues like the Executioner or busy himself with a Great Work like Pontanus. Once he had moved into the Tabernacle, he no longer went outside it, neither did he appear to take part in any of its ordinary tasks. He certainly talked, and talked almost incessantly. I was amazed that he could live in the same house as the Gold-Washer who loved the silence of the book-lice. Although he spoke only one sentence a day, if he began it in the morning he had still, late at night, not reached the end, so that he had to continue as soon as he woke in the morning.

Often he was interrupted. For his advice was asked on all sorts of problems, from the practical to the most personal. He, who was older than the other Gold-Washers, gave advice willingly, and his counsel was short, pithy and often also to the point, but after he had given his counsel he returned to his own sentence.

I never saw him take a step. Perhaps he was paralysed? In summer he sat in the French garden – for such a garden, too, was built in the Tabernacle – beside the fountain, in winter in a high-backed chair in a room with views in three directions. And from that chair flooded a stream of words and memories that ran under the earth in silence when there were no listeners present, but welled up audibly as soon as any ear was brought in by anyone's feet.

I never happened to see how he moved from one place to the other, but I suppose the others carried him.

What did he really speak about? Of course, I heard only fragments, no one heard anything but fragments. But it seemed to me as that he wanted to gather together into one and the same sentence everything he had experienced, to build from it a strong and compact whole, a Tabernacle of his own.

This sentence he sculpted and polished as the Executioner did his images, he examined it as the second Gold-Washer did his terrarium, watched over and guarded it as Pontanus did his bottle. The sentence was *his* pan, and the gold he washed in it was the meaning of his life.

'Why do you talk so much?' the Child of the Tabernacle once asked the Gold-Washer.

'Why?' the Gold-Washer asked, and interrupted his long sentence for a moment.

'But surely someone has to speak, since so many keep silence. Since animals cannot and gods do not wish to. I can and I wish to. And I have nothing else of my own but words, nothing else of my own.'

How to listen to Babel

He, too, was one of the Gold-Washers. Everyone knew him, for he went everywhere, was healthy, cheerful and attentive to everyone.

But nothing much was known about him. Not even which country he came from, for if one asked him about it, he pointed toward the south or nodded toward the east, or sometimes to the south-west. And at the same time he smiled a smile that was open and cheerful, the smile of a man who does not and cannot have any secrets.

Not even his official name was known. At first he was called the Man from Babel and later Mr Babel or just Babel. And Mrs Raa – after meeting him for the first time – said with a half-smile, in all sympathy: 'Well, look at that, there's Mr Good-as-Gold himself.'

Whatever language was spoken to him, the one which was generally spoken in the country or something more distant, he always seemed to understand what was being said, but his own response was a bewildering muddle, Babel's own Volapük. Any recognisable language it was not, but mixed with it were expressions from countless languages, Germanic and Romance, Finno-Ugrian and Indo-European and perhaps even languages that have long since died.

At times it also seemed as if Babel had strung words together without inflecting them at all, at times that, by combining or splitting them, that he had given words quite peculiar under- or overtones.

A friend of the gypsies claimed that Mr Babel spoke their language, but when he brought a couple of them to Babel, they did not understand his speech any better than the others.

Once a certain linguist came, very eminent, looked sharply at Mr Babel and said: 'Count to ten.'

He consented quickly and willingly, as he did to everything that was asked of him. Those who were nearby fell silent and gathered around Babel to hear better.

Babel let fly fluently and audibly: 'Yks, to, tre, fier, cinco, sest, okto, nava, syn.'

Everyone looked at the linguist, who shook his head in disbelief.

'There were ten different languages there,' he said gloomily.

Babel spread his hands and inclined his head, so that everyone had to laugh.

The laughter of some, however, had an angry undertone. Perhaps they believed that Babel was mocking them. Babel? Could there be even a drop of treachery in him? Such a warm-hearted, transparent man, who took part in everyone's joys and sorrows, who leaped from place to place, as lively as a squirrel, always good-tempered... But Babel had a human heart.

He was seen everywhere and invited everywhere. Wherever weddings were celebrated, exhibitions opened, long evenings spent in conversation, Mr Babel was also seen. He took part in every event with equal enthusiasm, inclining his ear in every direction and allowing his tongue, his countless tongues, to sing.

When I had already met Babel many times at different events, it began to happen that his speech left after-sounds in my ear. When, in my memory, I listened to his words, it began to seem to me that I understood a few details, a fragment here and there. But Babel's words had no connection with the event at which they were spoken. They seemed to be from some language's elementary primer, except that they were knotted together from the words of a number of different languages.

Why on earth had he said to Mrs Raa in the canteen of the

City Theatre, as he smilingly handed her a cup of coffee: 'Water is as important as it is pleasant'?

This is, of course, a translation, and Babel spoke very quickly and indistinctly, but nevertheless I do not believe that I am entirely mistaken. His words took on such a meaning in my ears, at any rate. But when I asked Mrs Raa what Babel had been talking about in the canteen, Mrs Raa said: 'Terrorism. Or was it vaccination? What a nice person he is.'

When, some weeks later, I met Babel in passing at the tram stop, he whispered something into my ear. I strained my attention and, to my bewilderment, thought I heard the following: 'The horn is a wind instrument. A bull's horn is strong. I have just visited the ironing woman.'

But there was also another way of listening to Babel, I realised that before long. One had to abandon all efforts, all attempts to understand, and simply give oneself up to his words as if one were lying on a jetty with the water whispering between the posts, as if one were leaning against a tree whose crown was shaken by the wind, as if one were to awaken suddenly after a quick dream and the city was murmuring behind curtains like a distant fun fair.

As long as one did not try to understand, as long as one merely looked at Babel's twinkling eyes so that his singing note began to rock one's head like a cradle, then it began to seem as if one understood everything, or at least the essence of what Babel wished to say. And then I, like many other of Babel's acquaintances, began to nod to him, to say a word or two myself, and Babel seemed to understand exactly what I meant.

And quite soon I was already sure that, whatever Babel was chattering about as he looked me in the eyes with his lovable smile, it was precisely, exactly what I had secretly thought to myself, but had simply not been able to express as eloquently, as vividly, as Mr Babel, one of the Gold-Washers.

Kinswoman Ouroboros

The Kinswoman was never counted as one of the Gold-Washers, even though she seemed to live permanently in the Gold-Washers' house. But no one had ever been less like their room than the Kinswoman.

The Kinswoman was the embodiment of everything I would like never to become. Who was she, really? The Gold-Washers always just called her the Kinswoman, but I do not know whether she was really related to any of them. I never succeeded in hearing her true name. I believe there was no one on earth who remembered, not even the Kinswoman herself.

For she forgot even what had happened the day before and where she lived and with whom. The Kinswoman no longer owned anything, not even her own past. She no longer had any manners, any appearance, any memory, any critical faculty, any skills or characteristics that might have drawn others to her. Perhaps she had only ever had a few of them, perhaps she had lost their last traces little by little, one at a time.

The Kinswoman was a stripped person; only wrinkles and bent, brittle bones were left. She could not rid herself of them, even though she often tore off all her clothes and wandered naked around the Tabernacle.

Or of her whims or her bad temper.

The Kinswoman could growl like a mongrel and neigh and cackle. She concealed the sounds of all the domestic animals in her palate. Sometimes she also burst into a shrill flood of abuse whose reason or object was difficult to make out. When the Kinswoman was content, she sang or whistled – tunelessly, always at the same pitch.

But the Kinswoman and her whistling were tolerated at

the Tabernacle. She was made as comfortable as possible, and she was served as if the Gold-Washers were bound to her by a secret debt.

'Perhaps it is the case,' Pontanus once said, 'that without the Kinswoman there would be no Tabernacle.'

'Do you mean,' I asked in astonishment, 'that the Tabernacle was built with her money? Is the Kinswoman rich?'

'Don't be stupid,' said Pontanus. 'As far as I know, the Kinswoman is poor as a church mouse. But without the Kinswoman, the Tabernacle would not be the Tabernacle.'

I did not understand Pontanus, and I never learned to like the Kinswoman. Often I left the room when she shuffled in. For when I looked at her I was afraid I would see the spectre of my own future.

I noticed that it was easier for me to bear her presence if I thought that she was, in one way or another, to blame for her state – her decrepitude. She had received a punishment – perhaps well-deserved – for something that I would never do.

But it was impossible not to meet the Kinswoman if one wanted to visit the Tabernacle. For she took part in every event, she sat in the best seat at the dining-table and she was served first.

When the Kinswoman woke from her afternoon nap, she would cry: 'Mother! Father!'

And one of the Gold-Washers would always get up and go to the Kinswoman's room and was mother and father to her.

The Kinswoman cast a long shadow on the walls of the Tabernacle. Harmless and thin as she was, an indefinite threat always wafted into the room when she stepped over the threshold.

Her behaviour was unpredictable. Sometimes the Kinswoman behaved like a respectable lady: she hung a cameo round her neck and offered the bread-basket to her neighbour at table, praised the taste of the fish. Then, without warning, she would begin to neigh like a bolting stallion, snatch a delicacy from her neighbour's plate and upset her own portion on to the table-cloth. The guests tried not to notice what had happened and to continue their conversation, but often their words broke off and their smiles froze.

'Dear Kinswoman,' said one of the Gold-Washers, 'perhaps you would prefer some shellfish salad.'

Then the Kinswoman was served with shellfish salad, and for a moment she looked favourably at the table-guests and wanted to raise her glass.

Once a concert was arranged in the Tabernacle. It included a première by the Gold-Washer with the hat, a concerto for bullroarers and bowed harp, three wine-glasses and typewriter.

In the middle of the performance, the Kinswoman came in, stark naked, grinning broadly with her gums. The withered bags of her breasts sagged to her waist. She threw one of them over her shoulder and pushed the other into her own mouth. Her wrinkled vulva had been shaved hairless. She had torn hair from her head so that she was now half-bald. She set herself in the centre of the room, her breast in her mouth, and looked at us like a baby.

It was a provocation!

'Doesn't the Kinswoman feel the cold?' shouted the composer of the sonata over the tapping of the typewriter and the clinking of the glasses. (I was to clink them when the Gold-Washer gave the sign.) 'Wouldn't the Kinswoman like this shawl for her shoulders?'

No, she would not. She had come as she was, and she wished to remain among us in that state. Then the Gold-Washer loosened his grip on the bull-roarers for a moment and brought an armchair for her from another room. There the Kinswoman sat, her knees drawn up, still nursing herself from her empty breast, which milk had surely never filled.

'Ouroboros,' Pontanus whispered to me, nodding toward the Kinswoman.

He meant the snake that ate its own tail, and whose picture hung on Pontanus's work-room wall.

The Kinswoman was, in the same form, mother and suckling child and Ouroboros.

Looking at her while tinkling the wine-glass and listening to the bullroarers and the tapping of the typewriter, I felt I had seen her somewhere else.

I remembered it as the Gold-Washer smashed one of the wine-glasses: it had been in a museum, far away in Europe. She languished there on a bronze pedestal in an uncomfortable position. She was naked there, too, and her appearance was that of a carcass dug from a grave. There the Kinswoman, too, had a name: she who was once the beautiful wife of the kettle-mender.

The meadow of humanity

'I have noticed,' said the Gold-Washer who loved book-lice, 'that Pontanus believes in people. I mean people as a possibility, a prelude and a stepping-stone. Poor Pontanus. He really is a heretic.'

'Aren't heretics people who don't believe?' I asked.

'Not now,' said the Gold-Washer. 'Now heretics are those who believe.'

We were sitting in a room like a coffer, long and narrow. But one could see out of it, and in two directions, for both walls were full of windows.

A shower of rain had gone over, the City of the Golden Reed sparkled and shimmered. Its reflections patterned all faces indoors, too. And outside the summer trees ran all the way along the boulevard to the shore, but people's houses looked into the street shadows.

Before us sat, peacefully, a great beast of the savannah: a lady wearing a leopard-patterned coat and a leopard-patterned scarf and leopard-patterned boots. The room swayed past the cathedral and over a bridge and across a square that was swarming with people.

'What value can there be in something that is so numerous?' asked the Gold-Washer, who was looking out of the window at the ceaseless motion of feet, the hustle of insect-like running. 'For all that is plentiful is cheap. All that is over-abundant is harmful.'

Strange that it should be a Gold-Washer who said so, the Gold-Washer who loved book-lice. There were many of them, too, they had spread everywhere. If one looked at the ground and bent blades of grass and overturned stones, one could not avoid finding book-lice.

But it was clear that here, in the relationship between

value and quantity, was the question of his life, or one of them.

There was a stop and the leopard disappeared, but in her place sat another woman, who was covered in the hide of an unborn lamb.

'Is she crying?' I asked.

For it looked as though she was. There was no sound, but her shoulders shook under the lambskin until we reached the emperor's statue. There she rose and went past us to the central door. But look! Then we saw that her face was twisted, in thousands of creases, not from weeping but from laughter!

'It takes all sorts,' said the Gold-Washer dejectedly, and raised his sombre eyebrows.

'If you take them in your tweezers,' I said to the Gold-Washer, 'then who will survive?'

Then my gaze fastened itself upon the bench opposite. What a creature! He terrified me. In almost every respect, he was different from anyone else I knew. Surely he was not really a proper person. He was a fake, that was it! But if I am asked to describe him, my words curdle and break.

His face – well, some would call it a face, but not I. To me it was a fen, a swamp, quicksand, that swallowed up gazes. But there were eyes in that marsh, got from God knows where, and what eyes...I refuse to describe them more closely, for it was the eyes that – once and for all!

There is little to say of his clothes, he was wearing clothes like the others, human clothes. And there was hair on his head, shoes on his feet, but they did not help – one could even say: they revealed him even more glaringly, they were so clearly parts of a *false costume*.

It seemed to me that the creature who was sitting opposite had finally denied his humanity, abandoned it or sold it. Now he was merely pretending to belong to the same species as the others who sat in the carriage. His eyes gave him away. No observation could make them stir. Absent from them was the fluid, living gold of consciousness, which Pontanus expected to develop in his bottle.

I looked at the Gold-Washer, but he did not appear to have noticed anything. What if there had been a conductor in the carriage, would that individual have been allowed in at all? The officials of the local transport service are exact in their duties. They carry only people and lapdogs.

My gaze returned to him again and again. If one looks at such a phenomenon too earnestly and for too long, one can catch an infection. Did I?

It felt as if I had when we returned to the Tabernacle, to the other Gold-Washers. I wondered whether I recalled him who I felt was no longer a person.

And in the evening I went to Pontanus and watched him work in order to forget my own state. It smelled there, but I did not care. Pontanus was calculating something, I watched the dance of his large hands on the keyboard.

'Pontanus, do you believe that I – that I, too, am a person, I mean: a real person?' I asked as if in passing.

He glanced at me absent-mindedly in the midst of his calculation and then turned back. Only after a moment did he ask: 'Do you doubt it?'

'I do,' I confessed to him. 'I feel as if I were something else.'

'In that case, you are,' he said.

'A person, you mean? A real person?'

'For a person is always something else,' Pontanus said. 'He is neither this nor that, neither here nor there, neither good nor evil. Like a particle, whose position cannot be defined.'

'Be careful,' said the helmeted Gold-Washer, who was standing in the doorway, his hands in his pockets. 'Don't believe him. He'll find a place for you, sure enough. Before you notice what is happening, you will be in a bottle being sublimated and distilled and desiccated.'

But I sat in Pontanus's room all evening.

I was once more like a grain in an ear of corn, and when the wind blew from the sea over the city, the grains rustled, and there was a field of people, a golden meadow of humanity, which yielded, stem by stem, ear by ear.

Left and right

The torsos

There were often parties at the Tabernacle, for one reason or another, at all times of year. But I seem to remember that they took place most often in the autumn, as on one occasion when Mrs Raa arrived late at a feast in the Tabernacle.

The cloudy day was motionless over the city, and the Pantheon was dim. The semicircular niches, which had been empty on Mrs Raa's previous visit, now had several inhabitants. The Executioner had carved more oddities: a cat-mummy and a basilisk, a monopod and an androgyne, a Ziz bird and a four-faced woman who had eight arms, like a winged wheel.

In the last wall-niche, closest to the door that led to the saloon, stood a large torso, the figure of a youth which was, unlike the others, so vividly and naturalistically carved that it looked like flesh and blood. It had a serious face, a bald, handsomely shaped head and a naked upper body, slim and firm, but the sculptor had clothed its lower body in blue jeans. Both the arms of the sculpture were broken off just below the upper arm.

'Wait!'

A deep, soft voice halted Mrs Raa just as she was about to open the door that led to the saloon. But the hall was empty, apart from the wooden oddities; neither, as she glanced back, could she see anyone at the outer door.

Then the Torso leaped, smiling, down the few steps that had been built in front of each wall-niche (as if all the inhabitants could come and go as the fancy took them) and approached her, smiling companionably.

Mrs Raa took a step backward. Of course, as she retreated, she already understood that the statue had, naturally, not come to life, but that before her stood a real man. But it would have been easier for her to confront a speaking statue than a person who had been so terribly mutilated.

Why was he standing in the niche? Mrs Raa could not immediately think of a reason, but the question remained in her mind all evening, as black and as unyielding as the figures in the niches.

Mrs Raa had offered her hand before she remembered what she had first noticed: there was no hand for her to shake. Her hand dropped at once, but the boy had already noticed her gesture, and his smile changed: it became tainted and dimmed.

Mrs Raa remembered now: she had known the boy when he still had all his limbs.

She saw the boy under another sky, offering coins to an ice-cream vendor, throwing a ball on a sports field, dragging his mother's shopping bag with both hands.

'What has happened to you?' she was unable to stop herself from whispering.

'An accident,' the Torso replied shortly and shrugged his handsome shoulders, whose continuation was merely the dim air. The amputation had been done neatly, as if with two strokes of an axe, and apparently long ago; the scars had faded.

Mrs Raa wanted to ask why no artificial arms had been made for the boy. Very willingly she would have thrown some garment across the Torso's shoulders to cover the stumps of his arms, but she was not wearing anything superfluous. And she knew, knew from the Torso's expression and stance and nakedness, that this would have been the worst insult; the Torso did not want artificial limbs or clothes. He wanted to appear to people just as he was: a torso.

The boy came closer, as if he intended to tell Mrs Raa something else, perhaps connected with the accident, but at that moment they heard behind them running steps. It was the Glass-Girl. She did not appear to notice Mrs Raa, but she grasped the Torso by the waist and drew him aside and began excitedly to whisper something to him, something to which the boy seemed to listen impatiently and silently.

Mrs Raa went to look for the Gold-Washers, but throughout the evening she bumped into the Torso in different rooms, on the terrace, in the pavilion and by the artificial ruin. Even at the dining-table, she could not resist glancing from time to time at how the Glass-Girl, who had whispered in the hall, gave food and drink to the Torso, who had not covered his upper body even for dinner.

'Will you have some?' asked his girl-friend again and again, although she had already filled the Torso's plate to overflowing. But the Torso ate little, and appeared to become more and more impatient and sombre.

No one who looked at the Torso at the great feast of the Tabernacle wanted to see him, but the Torso had deliberately positioned himself in the light of the brightest lamp.

There he sat, bearing his deficiency before him with the hands he did not have. He himself remained in hiding so that they did not see him; they saw only what was absent. And when they saw it, they were afraid.

Suddenly the thought crossed Mrs Raa's mind: 'At least he doesn't have to think what to do with his hands.'

And she was ashamed. To her astonishment, Mrs Raa began to discern in herself something like a dawning anger. As if she had wanted to shout: 'It's not true! You're making a bad mistake!'

For she felt that the Torso was forcing her to remember what has to be forgotten. Health was oblivion, but the Torso wanted them to remember because he had had to learn to remember. He wanted to force them to acknowledge their bodies, to believe that they themselves were bodies. And his mutilated nakedness was an ultimatum which they accepted because they could do nothing else.

And all the things they did when their eyes strayed to him; and when they quickly withdrew once more – leaned their heads on their hands, lit cigarettes, stirred their soup with a spoon, slapped a friend on the shoulder so that the wine splashed in the glass – or when they drew absent-mindedly with their finger on the table-top, they did it in the knowledge that the Torso would never do the same.

But with the Torso before her eyes, Mrs Raa remembered her life. It emerged like flotsam amid the tumult of other facts for just long enough for her to recognise it and admit – 'That's mine' – before it sank into oblivion once more.

And then Mrs Raa could not but acknowledge that the others, too, with their gloves decorated with winged wheels, were like the Torso, and still more torso-like than the Torso. That their torso-ness – although it was not as striking as that of the boy without arms – laid bare its withered stumps each autumn day when they could have unfastened and lifted, carried and cradled, worked and touched, but did not.

The secret

There is also a child in the Tabernacle. How is it that I had not noticed him at once? Short, hair like mist, dressed in red overalls. Had he always lived in the Tabernacle?

Now I saw him everywhere. His slender, playful form hurried like a will-o'-the-wisp through all the rooms of the Tabernacle, Pontanus's chamber and the Kinswoman's rose-room, the Pantheon, the courtyard and the pavilion. He flashed through the landing, but immediately rose into the air, speeded by the swing.

When I hastened inside, he stood in front of me and asked: 'Who are you?'

I told him my name as if that were an answer. He ran away without hearing all of it. I was a little disappointed, as if I had expected the child to give a better answer to his own question.

Seeing his narrow back, I remembered how I had once thought adults were keeping a great, unimaginable secret. I wanted to grow up soon so that I could learn it. Then, at last, I would know why people lived and how. Then – I believed – all the curtains would open and all the stage-sets would be moved aside. Every day would be an answer, as bright as a mother's face.

But now, as the Child of the Tabernacle ran on his way, it looked as if it was he who was the keeper of the secret, so light and fast and sure was he.

This secret could not be spoken, but it was apparent at every moment as the Child moved through the Tabernacle, laughed and talked, ate and played.

But after the visit of the Torso the Child changed; it was as if he became immersed in his own thoughts. Day after day I saw him, between his games, looking at his hands, turning them before him, putting them together, spreading his fingers and squeezing his hands into fists. A strange child.

Until once the Child went to the Gold-Washer who always sat inside his endless monologue. When the Gold-Washer turned his gaze on the Child, he interrupted his own work.

'Tell me why I have these hands,' asked the Child of the Tabernacle.

I heard his question and pitied him. I was wrong in imagining that he had the secret in his possession. For the Child was one of those who do not feel anything in the world to be their own, not even their hands, their feet, their eyes. What others put to use immediately, self-evidently, they grasp timidly, and cannot hold on to anything. They have nothing, nothing; but their poverty is a whole continent, just risen from the water.

But the Gold-Washer, too, looked at his own hands and said, remembering the Torso: 'If you had no hands, you would know why.'

The phantom

All the same, the Torso had arms. They were invisible arms, and he could not grasp anything with them, or embrace or hit. But they definitely existed – although only for him, personally – for they ached almost incessantly. Any other evidence of the existence of his arms was not vouchsafed to the Torso; but it was enough.

These immaterial arms hung limply by the Torso's sides and he could not influence their activity with his will. Even if he had bellowed 'Rise!' at them with all his strength – and his voice was as resonant and deep and metallic as a trombone – they would not have moved.

To begin with, after the accident, the Torso's phantom arms had been the same in every respect as his former, bodily arms. The only difference was that no one could see them. But with the months and years, the phantom arms began to shrink. It was as if they were withdrawing into him, becoming reabsorbed by the stumps of his arms. Now he felt that his elbows had already risen almost to the level of his lungs. The Torso sometimes wondered when he would feel his palms and long fingers straggling from his upper arms.

'And what will that look like,' the Torso thought. 'Like a fish's fins.'

But as soon as he had thought this, the Torso remembered that it would not look like anything at all.

When his arms had finally been reabsorbed into him, would the pain stop? Or would yet a third pair of arms appear from somewhere?

'Let me massage them,' said the Glass-Girl sometimes. She noticed when the Torso's arms were aching, although he never complained.

'Massage what?' asked the Torso, and laughed maliciously.

But sometimes, if the pain was so nerve-racking that the Torso's invisible hands existed more than everything that was left between the left and the right – his visible body – the Torso allowed the Glass-Girl to touch him. Or not him, but the air at his sides.

'Here?' the Glass-Girl asked shyly.

Did the Torso's ghostly hands feel the caressing touch of the Glass-Girl's fingers? Not really, for there was no sensation in them but their own pain. But from the Glass-Girl's light fingers flowed a warmth that turned away the most nerve-racking hook of the pain.

'If I could, I would graft my own hands on to you just like new branches are grafted on to apple trees in spring,' the Glass-Girl said once.

'You shouldn't do that,' the Torso said. 'How do you know what I would do with them? I'm not trustworthy, don't even think about it. You don't know the first thing I'd do wouldn't be to strangle you with your own hands.'

As soon as he had said this, and when the Glass-Girl had turned, silenced, toward the door, the Torso felt once again that where his self ought to be there was only an empty space separating those two, right and left, from each other. And *they* were real, while what was between them was mere desolation.

Such was his body: the branchless trunk of a non-existent tree.

And this understanding wounded the Torso so painfully that he called the Glass-Girl and she turned. With a new humility in his voice, the Torso asked: 'Would you give me my wallet?'

Knowing well what was being demanded of her, the Glass-Girl obediently took the wallet from the back pocket of the Torso's trousers, opened its side section and took from it a small, flat box.

'How many?' the Glass-Girl tonelessly, without looking at the Torso.

'Two, no – give me three,' said the Torso, opening his mouth in preparation like a young bird.

Soon, very soon, a different atmosphere spread around the Torso. Something had changed both around him and within him – all because of a few shiny capsules. He knew the change would not last, but it was real none the less; almost as astonishing as if something reminiscent of gold had condensed itself from Pontanus's reeking brews...

The Torso did not notice that the Glass-Girl had long since left. The banging of a brush was heard from the next room; the Glass-Girl was cleaning there.

From room to room she moved in the draughty mansion of the Tabernacle, searching one corner after another, as if by tidying them she could also brighten the Torso's gloom. As if she could find what she sought *there*: the miracle that would turn the Torso's indifference into love, the tender flame that would warm his coldness to a glow and make of suffering the bread of life.

Such was the Glass-Girl's Great Work.

Colour or ash

The cap of good fortune

Sometimes the cap of good fortune descended on to my head. I believe the Gold-Washer's iridescent hat was related to my own extraordinary headdress.

It was not mine, of course; I was merely allowed to carry it for a few moments, like a princess her diadem. I do not know where it came from and why it came to my head in particular, neither could I predict when it would appear. Suddenly it was simply there, a covering for my hair; I felt with my scalp, my temples, its light, sweet weight, as if a caressing hand had been left forgotten on my head.

But it was not a hand, nor anything human. For the moment it lingered on my head, I felt secure, as if I were sheltered by all-enveloping, warming, elastic armour. I was immune to sudden strokes of destiny, invisible demons who sought their victims from house to house, quarter to quarter. And, more astonishing still: not even time or its vassals could tyrannise me when I bore on my head the cap of good fortune.

I recognised the shimmering gaze that I saw in my own mirror-eyes always when I wore the cap of good fortune. The Torso looked around him in the same way when the Glass-Girl put two or three white capsules on his tongue. This gaze, it seemed to me, was bright enough to change and make new, to clean and ennoble everything it touched. As the owner of the cap of good fortune, I was even convinced that I could never again be unhappy or ill. I knew then that joy is the state for which human beings are born and in which they are meant to live and die.

The cap or skullcap pressed more tightly against my eyebrows and my skull began to experience pleasure all over. It was localised but it belonged to the entire organism, like sexual pleasure. Strong, wise, and with sovereign pride I looked around me: the square was paved with precious stones, and a flaming mirror had been raised against the sun. It was a high building whose western side was nothing but sunset windows.

Every word I heard then resonated in my skull like the sound of a wonderful instrument.

'It is beautiful,' said the woman beside me at the meat counter of the supermarket as the shop assistant held out a joint of meat for her to see.

And the woman was right: anything as beautiful as that juicy red lump, bloody, fresh, had hardly been seen.

A strange pleasure! What was its origin? What was its destination? Its rapid current, which sped me along in its foam as I sat, peaceful and independent, at the marble table of a café and watched the progress of a ray of sunshine on the green frond of a palm, washed the shores of both day and night.

Perhaps Pontanus's dry water swirled in its eddies, for I never got wet from its spray or drowned in its waves.

Poor Pontanus. In my own state of immortality, his efforts and his Great Work seemed more futile than ever before. For all had already been given; that, too, for which I had not remembered to ask. I had no debts, no dues. I was permitted to rest in the golden seedcase of the world in gratitude and praise.

If there is such a thing as the Holy Spirit, did not the cap of good fortune pour it over me? Did it not show itself in the meaning that filled everything I perceived? A meaning that glowed with the colours of a peacock like a hot summer's day, like summer at its height...

How their enchanting fan refreshed my gaze, wherever I looked: at the earth or at the sky, at people's clothes or into their eyes, at carved or uncarved wood, at the solitude of my own room or at the stones of the street, trodden by all.

The lens

A friend, whose name I do not now happen to remember, lived in another town. It was a small coastal town, beautiful and old. In summer it was visited by many travellers, for a deep, narrow bay penetrated into its centre, an ideal harbour for yachtsmen.

There must have been a time – years ago – when I, too, visited it every summer.

My friend lived alone some distance from the centre of the town, on the side of a hill. About his house I can now say only that it had a wooden balcony with a direct view of the bay. Indeed, all other recollections flee headlong from the flickering light of my memory.

We stood on the balcony side by side – or perhaps my friend was slightly behind me, but I leaned on the rail and drank in the evening's landscape with my eyes, one draught after another.

Coloured lamps had been lit on the piers and shoreline boulevards as if a great feast were approaching, and their reflections rippled in the clear water. But the western sky had not completely dimmed, either; a glowing strip threw its golden reflection over the whole town, and over us, up here on the balcony.

And then I felt again a touch on my hair.

My god, how happy I was! – just as if the gold came from us ourselves, up here on the balcony... As if we, our own eyes, had reflected drinkable gold into the water, on to the town, on to the dizzying sky's last shore.

I never remembered having seen a view to match it... Joy, which had flickered miserably for long years, received new fuel from the glow in the west and now burst into tall flames.

But my friend, whose name I still cannot recall, did not share my admiration. Then I did not ask the reason, for I outstripped his mood with the wind of my own indescribable joy. I wanted somehow to record the moment that was so great, and thought: I shall take a photograph of the view! At once I turned to my friend, whose name I do not remember, and asked to borrow his camera.

Well! There he stood, with his camera in his outstretched hand, as if he had at once divined my intention.

I raised the viewfinder to my eyes and passed it along the horizon and the surface of the water. But did my eyes deceive me? Where now were all the colours? I could no longer see hundreds of coloured lanterns, the mirror of the water did not shimmer and the sunset had vanished. I saw only a burnt-out, ash-coloured landscape, and a single streak of blood in the western sky above it.

Now the viewfinder was angled so that I could see only water through it. It was like this: I no longer saw water rippling in the lights, I saw beneath the surface. It was dark and leaden like the sky, but transparent none the less. And there, beneath the water, surrounded by the town and the harbour, rested two immense beings.

They lolled side by side, and their broad carcasses covered the entre bottom of the bay from one shore to the other. One of them lay on its back so that its white belly showed; to me it looked like a cross between a pig and a fish. The trunk of the other was more reptilian; it recalled a leguana or the tuatara of the Tabernacle, but much bigger.

I did not regard the couple with shock or horror, but an immense stupefaction made the camera so heavy that it slipped from my hand on to the balcony floor.

I made no move to lift it. The bang was audible, perhaps something broke, too, probably the lens. But my friend, whose name I still simply cannot remember, did not seem even to notice what had happened. He stood motionless, his arms hanging by his side, and his unfocused gaze was dusted with the same ash as the evening sky. We did not exchange a single word, but I knew he knew.

My head was bare, the cap of good fortune had gone. I was once more at the mercy of chance and necessity.

But I simply cannot any longer remember even the features of my friend's face, or even whether he was clothed or naked. And where his face should be I see only a misty oval, as featureless as Venus covered by cloud.

Prisoners of glass and mirror

The triumphal fanfare of Yikuhatsa

There was a great deal of glass in the Tabernacle. There were many windows, and they were large. On autumn evenings, when all lights were burning, the Tabernacle was as transparent as Pontanus's bottle or the Gold-Washer's terrarium.

Pontanus was visiting the book-lice in the room of the Gold-Washer who was writing about the past, significance and fate of the book-louse.

On the window-sill was a large and carefully tended terrarium. The Gold-Washer had gone to a great deal of trouble to transform the glass vessel into a landscape worthy of the book-lice. There was a hillock covered in a thin layer of new grass. There was forest – a couple of sword ferns, and a blue lake in a squat plastic cup. There was a steep cliff on which the book-lice were able to practise alpine climbing, and boulders in whose crevices they could sleep through the hottest moment of the day.

'Neither people nor book-lice –' said Pontanus, who had bent down to follow the insects' activity. Two lice were gnawing at a third, which was still wriggling.

We awaited the continuation of the phrase in vain. From another room, the whistling of the Kinswoman could be heard and, behind it, the silence of the chess-players.

'– nor the tuatara,' Pontanus said. 'All of them are only trials. Experiments, endless variations. They take time, a long, long time, and the experiments may seem cruel, but' (his finger rose) 'they are necessary. For another age will dawn. It will develop from this age like a caterpillar from its chrysalis.'

'Perhaps,' said the Gold-Washer. 'But whether it will be a better age, that we don't know.'

'Time will tell,' said Pontanus. 'The millennia will decide.'

'They will decide in favour of the book-louse,' said the Gold-Washer. 'We shall go the way of the dinosaurs, but the book-louse will go on haunting the earth's crust. And if that happens, it will be because it must happen.'

'Come,' said a Gold-Washer who stood, panting, on the threshold, on his head a worn-out hat. When he opened the door, they smelled smoke. 'Over there – on the waste heap – oh! an amazing fire!'

They all went out to look. The smoke seemed to be floating down the cordilleras of waste, but in fact the fire was not there, but much farther off. The sky glowed red over the southern half of the City of the Golden Reed, and the windows of the Tabernacle were blazing. They heard the sound of sirens.

The ravens of Edom were there, too. They sat on a sofa that had been carried out into the courtyard, dressed in their best clothes, as if attending a first night. The distant red touched their foreheads, too, and made them younger by years, by decades.

'Something terrible is happening there, I know it,' the Glass-Girl said. 'Assassinations. Arson. Massacres.'

'Sit down,' said the Gold-Washer. 'Look at them. They know how to get the best out of this.'

Between the ravens of Edom sat an old Gold-Washer, who was continuing his lifelong sentence:

'even if he never admitted it was true, there was not a doubt as to what was really going on, although it must be admitted frankly that none of us at that time understood that even he – in those difficult circumstances . . .'

'Vittere tele!' Babel shouted. He had climbed a little way up the side of the waste heap and was gazing through a pair of binoculars.

'What did he say?' Latona asked Pontanus.

'He said it's a fine view.'

'Not in the least,' countered a Gold-Washer. 'He said the

flames of hell warm us so sweetly. He said that without hell we would all freeze.'

'Is the whole city on fire? Shouldn't we do something?' the Glass-Girl asked, and coughed.

'Absolutely,' said a Gold-Washer. 'Bring my glass harmonica and take the bull-roarers for yourself. You, Latona, can fetch the bowed harp.'

In a moment the Gold-Washer announced: 'The name of this piece is the Triumphal Fanfare of Yikuhatsa.'

And, rotating his glass harmonica under the red sky, the Gold-Washer joined his triumphal fanfare to the simple, disconsolate song of the sirens.

Sediment

'In my bottle,' said Pontanus to the turbaned Gold-Washer, 'spring and summer and autumn and winter alternate. It is the universe in five decilitres. Matter within it changes in the same way as matter outside. When I look into the bottle, I see what happens to you and to me.'

'What happens to us?' the Gold-Washer asked.

'You know it all,' Pontanus said. 'Birth and death, growth and copulation and resurrection.'

'Really, oh, *that*'s what you mean,' said the Gold-Washer.

Beside the scales on Pontanus's table they saw a pestle, a mortar and a small bar magnet, as well as a pastry-brush, which Pontanus used in handling his fine powders. He warned us not to move or open the bottles.

'The impurity must remain on the bottom,' he said. 'It must be left in peace.'

'What are you doing today?' asked the Child of the Tabernacle as a curtain of snow floated outside the window.

'I shall take four parts of antimony and two parts of iron and mix them together thoroughly.'

'What will you do next?'

'Then I shall add the Secret Fire and heat it.'

I was there, too, when the snow had melted, and saw his head bent over his work and his incipient baldness. Because the window was open to April, drop followed drop until night in a continual race. When the sun struck the bottle on the window-sill, it threw a crooked rainbow on the wall; it was pale, but it still contained all the colours.

'What are you doing today?' asked the Child of the Tabernacle.

'Today I shall wait.'

'What will you wait for?'

'For this mixture to turn white,' said Pontanus. 'There is nothing else to do.'

And the days fly by; very soon the autumn equinox is at hand.

'What are you doing today?' asked the Child of the Tabernacle.

'I shall dry this mixture,' said Pontanus, 'and pound it to a fine powder with the pestle. Then I shall take three parts of it and mix with one part of Sun, add a little Secret Fire and heat it again.'

'I can't make head or tail of this,' said the Gold-Washer, who stepped in with a crooked smile, wearing a tricorn hat.

'All the skill!' said Pontanus, raising his finger, 'is in differentiating between the fine and the rough. All the skill! For God's sake! Don't touch that bottle. The sediment must not be moved.'

The Gold-Washer set the bottle down carefully on the table and patted Pontanus on the shoulder.

'You certainly make an effort,' he said. 'Thank you for that, Pontanus.'

And the Gold-Washer raised his tricorn hat.

'You make an effort, although the days darken and speed away. For a Gold-Washer, life is too short and too simple. It is as cramped as your bottle. There is no progress to be seen, we simply wander back and forth and disturb the sediment.'

'You are wrong,' said Pontanus. 'But you must go now. For I must start the fermentation.'

'Let us go,' the Gold-Washer said. 'But carry on, Pontanus, carry on, carry on. What other difference is there between our lives and those of the book-lice except this futile labour, your toil, Pontanus, and my madness and this tricorn hat.'

The feasts of paupers continue.
Our glasses are filled with dregs.
So rarely does the peacock
show the brilliance of its tail.

As soon as the peacock turns,
grasp the moment now.
Take hold of its loveliest feather.
Take with you the whole rainbow.

The shattering path

'What on earth is she doing?' I asked Mrs Raa. Both our gazes were fixed on the Glass-Girl, who was moving among the guests, looking anxious, in her hand a brush and dust-pan.

'Don't you know where she got her name?' Mrs Raa asked. 'You can see for yourself what she's doing.'

It was true. The Glass-Girl was sweeping again. She slipped between the guests, reached out, bent down, and swept the floor with her brush here and there between the shoes and chair-legs.

It has to be said that it was not the best possible time for such an activity. The Glass-Girl's slow and uncertain way of moving recalled a person fumbling in a dark, unfamiliar room; she took each step as if she feared a trap.

Some guests lifted their shoes, smiled and moved out of her way, but others frowned and stood their ground without interrupting their conversations. Some paid no attention to her whatsoever.

'Who told her to do that?' I asked. 'In the middle of a party?'

'No one,' said Mrs Raa, who knew. 'Do you really still not know the Glass-Girl? Now she is having one of her turns again. Let us just be thankful she doesn't use a vacuum cleaner.'

Now the Glass-Girl had reached the corner where we were sitting on uncomfortable trelliswork chairs. They had been designed by the Executioner. She nodded vaguely to us, thinking of other things, apologised and bent to look under the chairs, one after the other.

'Have you lost something?' I asked.

But she replied with another question: 'Have you broken anything? Perhaps a glass?'

And she gestured toward the stemmed glass I held in my hand.

A most unexpected question. I, too, looked at the glass, doubtfully as if seeking a crack. It was a very good glass, clear and cold; the lights of the evening glittered in its frost.

'This one is certainly sound,' I said to the girl, and she said quickly: 'Yes, of course, perhaps *that* one is. But it looks to me as if there are splinters over there. As if something were glittering there.'

She was still staring into some corner underneath the chair. I got up quickly and moved my chair aside.

'Look. Nothing but dust.'

'But in it, it seems to me... Don't you see? Tiny little fragments, a little broken glass... It's no trouble, I'll just...'

And she grasped her brush and gracefully, with a charming and economical movement, swept the dust into her dust-pan. Relief flickered across her pale, clean face.

'Sit down,' said Mrs Raa. 'Rest a while. I'll bring you something.'

But she was already looking at another corner, her eyes narrowing, her brush still at the ready.

'In just a moment, thank you very much. I just have to... Just a moment... Goodbye!'

And in a moment she was far away, among the other guests, busy at work whose necessity she alone understood.

Later, when the evening was already far advanced, a bonfire was lit in the courtyard and the guests of the Tabernacle gathered around it.

Then I thought I heard a crackling that did not come from the fire. It had rhythm and weight, it came from footsteps. But never before had walking on sand given rise to such a sharp sound – it was as if someone had been crunching on hard bread.

I turned to see who had such a biting tread. I could distinguish the shape of the Glass-Girl, but now she did not have a brush. I saw her small face as a lantern in the light of the lanterns. But while the other lanterns had been hung in the trees to mark the Gold-Washers' territory in the night, her face flickered alone in the shade of the Tabernacle.

The Glass-Girl was walking away from me and away from the bonfire. I rose to call her. How could her footsteps, formerly so soft, so cautious, crunch so loudly in the frosty night of the Tabernacle?

But I did not call her; I fell silent when I saw the path on which she was walking. At first I thought that it was hoarfrost, that the ground was frozen. That her heels were crushing the surface of a puddle that had shrunk into a crust of ice.

Where was she going? In each of her footsteps there was both the crackling of the fire and the tinkling of ice, but now I could see more clearly: there was neither fire nor ice – she was treading pure glass, splinters, fragments. Her fear had combined with the sand like soda, and the secret fire that burned her in vain had ripened, in its kiln, a sparkling harvest. The Glass-Girl's path was now covered in broken glass; it shattered, tinkling, under her steps, and behind her opened the silver wake of her own fear.

How magically it sparkled and glittered!

What was seen in the knife

Ash-trays filled. Glasses and eyes emptied. Through the veil of smoke and buzz of conversation they pierced passages from one group to another, from the book-case to the window, from the superabundance of the tables to the centre of the floor, from the crush of the sofa to the solitude of the doorway. In this way they wove into the room a shimmering network, a force-field, that flexed and expanded with the warmth of their steps, their speech and their gazes.

Then the longing for a mirror began once more in Latona. She became absent-minded and could no longer bear to listen to the arguments of her father and a Gold-Washer, or to Babel's impassioned cries.

'It's a question of balance,' said her father. 'The right timing... so that the quintessence does not... not to mention control of temperature.'

'Watu wazuri,' said Babel. 'Vehosek – sermanahan...'

The Gold-Washer tried to catch her eye, but Latona herself could not meet his: her eyes had become mixed up with the flock of strangers' eyes.

How she yearned for her own eyes! But there was not a single mirror in the room, only empty walls and some strange pictures, such as the engraving above the sofa. It was framed, but it had no glass, no reflections.

Instead of her eyes, she saw a medieval city with three cubes floating in the air above the towers and bridges.

It was a long time, many hours, since Latona had last seen her own image. Her face must already have changed many times.

Was it vanity that now made her uncomfortable? Latona, the daughter of Pontanus, pressed her hands to her cheeks, but her fingers were blind; they did not tell her how she looked.

What had happened to her face during these unguarded hours? She felt she could no longer control it. In whose power was it? Perhaps it had already changed or aged unrecognisably. Perhaps it had become diseased, perhaps it had even been *infected* by another face that she had looked at, such as the Torso's or the Kinswoman's.

Latona felt as if she had, against her will, raised into the realm of the gaze strange expressions and insinuations that anyone at all could read and pick in passing.

Troubled, Latona wanted to wipe them from her skin, but ordinary water could not wash them off; she must bend over the surface of a mirror.

She looked at the window, seeking her own reflection, but it was still so early that the windows conducted gazes through them. Latona did not see her eyes; she saw only the Child of the Tabernacle, who was cradling his solitude, a black silhouette against the slanting spring light.

Latona looked at the tables and saw that the plates and glasses had already been cleared away. But on one of the side-tables was a cheese-tray, bottles and a knife that no one had yet used. It was serene, as clear as spring-water.

Latona walked up to the table and grasped the knife as though she intended to cut a piece of Tilsit cheese. She tilted it with quick fingers until the light shone on it and, relieved, she saw something pale and questioning, solitary and her own, something which hesitated and which was encircled by a glimmer of hair.

And when her hand moved, almost imperceptibly, the clean blade gave back first the drawing and a corner of the ceiling, then the back of the trellis chair and her father's stooped shoulder and forefinger and finally the Gold-Washer in his glittering top hat, who was calling to her with all his eloquence and all his mischievousness in the knife-bright distance of the room.

Sounds of the reed

The rattle

'Father,' moaned Latona, daughter of Pontanus. 'You will poison us or blow up the whole house.'

And she parted the curtains with an impatient gesture, and opened all the windows wide. And the raw and strong breath of the outdoor air, the distant sounds of the Golden Reed and the all-pervasive light of a winter's day, the colour of skimmed milk, made Pontanus's already austere face grow pale and his enterprises look more pointless than ever.

Sometimes, around midday, a strange, coarse rumbling reached the side of the Tabernacle from across the waste heaps. At the beginning I had once or twice stretched out of the window to see what caused it; later, I no longer wished to look.

I knew that a beggar wandered there, rummaging in the rubbish-heaps, who had some kind of rattle attached to the collar of his coat, a buzzer powered by batteries. An unpleasant cloud of noise surrounded him, like fear, wherever he shuffled.

'Perhaps he has a disease,' Pontanus said. 'Perhaps he wants to warn passers-by.'

Perhaps. I had seen the same spectre before, in the old churchyard. The sand and frost had been as hard as bone beneath my boots. The mossy, uneven flagstones had just been cleaned, the names and pious words engraved on them were visible to everyone once more, but no one stopped to read them.

Before me swayed the ugly apparition, exuding vapours of meths and urine; under his greasy jacket bare his chest showed. He secreted a noise, the whine of a buzzer, which mixed with the stench and was one with it. He looked as if he had risen from one of the graves beneath him and his sparse hair was sticky chaff, but his face he never showed.

His matted head lolled against his chest at an unnatural angle, as if the bones in his neck had been severed.

Buzzing incessantly, he reeled along the sandy paths that surrounded the flagstones, and an invisible power flown from the north tossed the tow on his head and the branches above it.

Had the same rattle not buzzed on the escalators of department stores and in queues in banks and government offices, in railway station tunnels and tram carriages, at fun-fair candy-floss stalls, within the white fence of the summer café? Its sound was like vengeance for an unremembered crime.

Rattle, buzzer, clatter away. Lift your head, rattle-carrier! Make your face to shine upon us. Who knows when it will be my turn to fix a buzzer to my breast, which still swells, which is made to tremble sometimes by caresses, sometimes by laughter and tears. Rattle, clatter! Guide us, show us what we fear, when we must give way. Do not fall silent, so that we may know where we do not want to go, so that we may point: that way lies evil, that way lies the chasm. If one can only avoid it, the danger is over, and everywhere else the roads of freedom wander.

But Pontanus closed the window.

What would he have answered had I asked him then, as I so often wished: tell me, tell me straight, are you absolutely serious? Do you believe in quintessences and the king and queen and that everything is alive? Or can you say still more, do you dare say you know?

If I had asked at a naked, everyday moment, a moment of the rattle, a moment of skimmed milk, when not a single thread of colour was reflected from the peacock's tail, would his eyes have avoided mine? Would he have risen from his table and extinguished the Secret Fire and left the room and the Tabernacle without a backward glance?

But I never dared ask, because I did not want him to bow his heavy head, because I wanted to believe that someone believed, at least one person in this rattle-city.

The sound of humanity

But the cry of the murderer sounded in our ears the longest of all.

It reached as far as the courtyard of the Tabernacle – which Pontanus called by so refined a name as *cour d'honneur* – from the other side of the waste heaps. There, on the northern side of the refuse dump, grew, or rather struggled to grow, a thick spruce wood.

It was a phantom forest, for the lowest branches of the spruces had shed all their needles, the saplings were mere trunks and the earth so trodden, hard clay, that nothing could germinate there any longer. But the clay brought forth bottle-shards, the earth's crust flowered with plastic bags bearing red letters.

Into this wood fled a boy who had killed his mother, raped a child, strangled a girl. His tracks smelled like toxic waste; dogs and motor-bikes growled at his heels. Barking and cries, the explosions of accelerating engines tore the ears of every Gold-Washer.

At last the boy had arrived. A steep cliff face cut off his escape, patrols encircled his panic.

Then from the murderer's throat there burst forth a whimper, there escaped a howl; the echo of his cry boomed from the cliff: 'Mother! Where is my mother? Mother will defend me.' And like an echo he was answered by the Kinswoman's weeping from the courtyard of the Tabernacle.

The Cougher

I did not see with my own eyes the boy who shouted for the mother he had murdered. He remained only a voice, like the Cougher, who lived in the City of the Golden Reed, on its public transport system.

How often I, too, used it to travel round this stony promontory, which protrudes into the sea like a forlorn finger testing the coldness of the water.

Often, when I stepped inside, all the seats were already taken and on the journey as many as one and a half times the permitted number of passengers crammed themselves in.

The proximity of strange bodies and strange smells was agonising enough, but in addition hands often appeared to torment me.

The hands appeared from the midst of the crush and lived a life of their own, feeling, touching, even slipping inside your clothes if your position happened to be suitable. They did not belong personally to anyone; they just materialised from the rustling coats and the static electricity of man-made fabrics.

On my last journey, I thought I felt again such a fumbling, greedy touch: I looked behind me, but saw only unstirring profiles and eyes that stared inward. And then the hatred in the conductor's voice, a real, living disgust, pushed me, too, forward, as she raged, in all the city's official languages: 'Move right down inside the car!'

Raincoats hissed, and there was an echoless cough. I pricked up my ears, was immediately on my guard: was the Cougher here?

Yes, he was here, but for a long time I was the only one who knew it. For all that had happened was something completely ordinary: someone had cleared his throat. He coughed once more, and then again, and again. But nothing opened, and the disturbance continued.

Such a thing can happen to anyone, of course. But this was only a foreword, a prelude.

For as everyone was sinking back into a daze of indifference, we were shaken by the first real outburst of coughing.

Where did it come from? From what blackened region, abandoned by angels? I heard the phlegm moving back and forth in the windpipe, wheezing and bubbling. I heard how it rose from soft, already decaying tissue, and everyone remembered, with a start, the secrets of their own guts.

Every fit of coughing hit its mark. There was nothing behind which to take shelter. The seminal fluid of a mortal illness was being sprayed on to us. And as series of explosions followed another, I heard behind them a tightening silence. Hands became fists, but their helplessness was unfathomable. I did not dare push my fingers into my ears, and how would it have helped: this cough was not heard with the ears, but with every muscle and nerve-fibre.

I know: the Cougher does not cough because he cannot help it, but because he wants to cough. He wants to blaspheme and dishonour his fellow-travellers. He wants to steal from us the air that we must breathe, this small, fusty, closed air-space. He wants to fill it with the tiny spores of his own ruin. And like a strange hand his cough gropes for a life that I believed to be my own.

Pity him? Who could demand that? Whoever has heard the Cougher even once cannot be so sanctimonious.

His cough has stormed his frothing slobber over my head: 'Since I must, so must you, too... Where I am, there shall you be!'

I have heard that cough, I have heard how it insults everything that, to me, means love and life and immortality. No, I do not pity him, for whoever coughs like that is not a real person. For those explosions would have torn him to shreds if he were an ordinary citizen. For he would long ago have drowned and suffocated in the Niagara of his own poison.

But he goes on, he goes on, for he is not a human being, but an incarnate plague, he is the Cough itself.

My God! In the bus, an unpleasant thought crossed my mind: what if he knows something about me, something I cannot remember, something so shameful that the accusation of his cough is completely justified? Was he, then, my accuser and my judge, and was my punishment the hollowness of his cough?

I stood in the crush at the front of the bus and, past a fur coat smelling of mothballs, I saw the driver crouched over his steering wheel. He was suffering, I could see it from his neck, his whitened knuckles. We were still on the bridge, the journey was continuing and the final stop loomed like a promised land on the far side of towers, squares, crossroads. It was a miracle, it was a mercy, that our bus, which the Cougher's fits of rage shook like a bottle, did not turn, shuddering, into the wrong lane and dash across the parapet of the bridge into the quiet of the canal, where even the Cougher would finally have been silenced.

Do you know what I wanted to do then? I wanted to push my way through the fur coats and the winter raincoats, bend over the driver and grab the dashboard. It was full of levers and switches and signal lights, and I would have tried all of them, one after another. For I felt, for a moment I was sure, that there must be a button which I could press to end this disturbance, which would have silenced the Cougher's drumfire.

There must be such a button there, there must be one somewhere, since there are levers at whose touch cities dissolve into emptiness and crowds puff into dust and whirlwinds of ash, spin and disperse like smoke into the silence of the night...

The gong

It's true, isn't it, that there are sounds that can empty, repel and neutralise other sounds? Such was the sound of the gong, it was as pure as the gold of Ophir. I turn the gong against people's talk, quarrels and rattling, against the cough and the howling of the murderer.

There was a time when I heard it again and again during the afternoon rush-hour, in the tumult of buying and selling, when people had heavy loads to carry and the sunset made the eyes of those who were hurrying home seem bloodshot. Boi-oing!

The whole street was streaming with faces, collars and hats, hair, scarves and overcoats, and they slipped forward like sails, carried by their own emptiness. Everyone else was anxious, everyone else was far from home, but he who came toward me was at home with every step, his destination was the moment of striking when brass flowered.

There he was, as anonymous as all the shadows of the street, slipping past me with his shaven head, around him the gold-brown wind of his cloak, lingering in his smile. His stick, too, I remember; there was a round knob at the top and it struck precisely, struck unhesitatingly like the hammer of fate and stopped at once, struck and drew away into the still quivering air, and in the iridescent colours of the windows flashed the brass of the gong.

What do you think, did he go round the entire city sounding out in the same way, so that not a single note arrived too early or too late, and so that he never sprained his bare ankles, which were encircled by the cords of a pair of sandals, even on the streets that were cobbled?

His blows were a thread which bound the whole city together, as if someone were to bend over and pick up from the paving-stones everything that had been forgotten, so that nothing should remain unconnected and alone any longer.

And if you, too, heard it, do you not regret that you did not do as you wished: that you did not dance after him, clapping your hands, clip and clap, whenever his stick boomed on the gleaming convex surface?

But although you only turned to look after him, bag in hand, did you not, in reality, go after him none the less, and did not someone else, and someone else again, and did we not together celebrate the fact that the city was, for once, single and united, whole, our own, and that it lived with all of us, without ever tiring throughout the moments of the day?

The silence of the meadow

The sun shone into the room, distant and low. It was the oblique unglowing gaze of a winter's day.

A grey squirrel was leaping about in the pine-tree beyond the window, amusing the Child of the Tabernacle. The others stayed inside and felt the cold, because the inhabitants of the Tabernacle felt the cold every winter. Its designers had forgotten the fourth season.

The tuatara had not been seen for some time. The ancient lizard was sleeping soundly in its den of a cardboard box in an empty room. All three eyes were closed, and one of the Gold-Washers had wrapped it in some red wool so that it would not feel the cold as they themselves did.

Pontanus came from his room to the stove, rubbing his hands.

'Things are going well,' said Pontanus. 'They're going very well. In a day or two I shall have reached the black stage.'

'Right,' said the Gold-Washer who was always present and always speaking, both aloud and silently.

'That's what he said in the spring,' said the Gold-Washer who loved book-lice. 'That's what he'll say next year.'

'Maybe he will,' said the first Gold-Washer. 'But the main thing is that he is making progress.'

We all fell silent, for the rumbling had begun again.

We heard it many times a day, for the Tabernacle lay under a busy flight-path. Above our heads people rushed eastward and westward, reading currency exchange rates and eating soft-boiled eggs, if it was morning. Sometimes the booming bellies of the aeroplanes seemed to touch the wings of the Tabernacle itself, as if to entice it, too, into flight. But the Tabernacle did not rise into the air, no, it just rattled and shook. As long as the building quaked, we could not speak, only wait.

And remember the summer's day when a bomb concealed in the hold had torn a hole in the side of such an aeroplane. We heard the explosion and all of us ran outside, everyone but the Kinswoman and the Gold-Washer who just sat and talked.

We saw the aeroplane tilt and lose altitude, but it carried on, it disappeared from view. Later we heard that it had landed at the airport of the Golden Reed exactly on schedule, even though there was a yawning rent in its body. But through the glare against which we shielded our eyes hurtled three or four packages. They were passengers who had been sucked out of the opening in the body and into the sunshine. It was the sun of a summer's day, but up there it was still terribly cold.

The noise of those masses of air! We saw them being thrown into the void, bound to their chairs. Quite certainly they had in their laps today's newspaper and a film-wrapped breakfast. Spinning, soundless as autumn leaves but much faster, they were torn away from their connection with humanity, from the unreal life they had prepared for themselves to the inhuman reality of death.

The top-hatted Gold-Washer spoke or pretended to speak to Latona, who was crouching by the fireplace in the stunning rumble. His mouth was moving, even his ears were moving, but there was no sound.

A summer pasture was dimly visible in the winter of the Tabernacle, the flowering side of a valley behind the refuse-hillocks. One of the aeroplane-seats had landed there, in the silence of the meadow, in the silence that returns after the worst has happened, the rumbling and the explosions and the tearing steel.

The passenger was still sitting, bound by his belt, but he was broken like a flower and the gaze of his eyes was detached, absent. In their emptiness, those unblinking eyes were like the sky; but they had no other perspective but its pure, glimmering blindness.

And the aeroplane had gone. They recovered their stolen voices, even the buzzing of a fly. It bounced against the windows of the Tabernacle, a little winter fly. For it could not know that the light toward which it struggled and strained was the brightness of snow and death.

Room for the soul

Sometimes I spent the night in the Tabernacle. Every night there was different, like every day in the Tabernacle. Sometimes I drank the mother's milk of dreams, rushing headlong from one image to another, farther and farther away from the house of the Gold-Washers and the book-lice.

But if I could not sleep, I could hear from below the squeaking of the bowed harp or the tinkling of the glass harmonica and, from time to time, strange cracks, as if the lash of a whip were striking thin skin.

On such nights, the solitude of the Gold-Washers filled the air of the Tabernacle with heavy secrets. I lay waiting for something, the splitting of the heart of night, the tearing of the curtain of the temple, the angel's trumpet. But nothing happened. The Tabernacle swam steadily, ploughing deep through the timeless night.

But around the time of the winter solstice, in the deep of the Tabernacle's night, I awoke to a hoarse bellowing. It was the kind of shout that cannot be suppressed, when torturing-irons break the leg-bone.

I put on my clothes, the door flew open as if of its own volition, and I fell down the stairs into the great common room. All the Gold-Washers were already there, but no one noticed my arrival. In their midst, the object of their undivided attention, swayed a narrow, dark tower. It was the old Gold-Washer, whom I had never before seen taking a single step. I had not guessed he would be so tall.

He was just standing, his shoes rooted to the ground, but swaying above like a tree on a hill. He stood and shouted: 'One must also leave room for the soul! Room for the soul!'

It was an entiely new and detached sentence. I wondered whether it was connected in any way with his long, lifelong sentence, which he had still been building the day before. Perhaps he had now reached the end of it. Perhaps a third sentence would follow soon.

Around the Gold-Washers I could see, at least, the Executioner and Babel and the Customs Man and the Gold-Washer who always wore a hat. But now he had no hat at all, so that he looked naked and even a little pitiable.

The others fell silent; only Babel was mumbling softly to himself, the language of Babel in his distress, the tongue of tongues, which each of us could understand, but no one could translate.

What could I have done? I was not needed there. I returned to the solitude of my three-cornered room, where the Gold-Washer's cry echoed once more: 'One must also leave room for the soul!'

Then peace returned. Not a sound was heard in the Tabernacle that night, in the house that was so big that there was even a room without walls, and another without a roof.

But not even that was enough. Nothing was enough for the soul, it was too big even for the pleasure palace of the Tabernacle.

The breath in our nostrils

He had heard that same sound countless times. It was the undercurrent of all the days, all the years, but only when the night deadened all the other sounds did this one – which was hardly a sound to begin with – rise so that the ear could hear it.

It was the first and it was the last, it belonged to everyone individually and it was everyone's in common, just as one and the same fire burns in cigarette lighters and pyres, grave-candles, flamethrowers and the coloured paper lanterns of August.

But this was not hot, but gentle as the touch of a beloved hand. To waken at night and feel on one's cheek, on one's bare shoulder its warm wind, passing through the nostrils of a child or someone one loves...

It took away all words – both trivial and weighty, disappointed and eager, cruel, tender, yearning, and the few words that were so simple and true that they could have been hewn into the bedrock, that same rock which one could not avoid treading wherever one went in the City of the Golden Reed.

The tide of life rose and fell with that wind, life's real, omnipresent spirit of truth.

In it were their inheritance and their possessions, received from the air, and it would disappear into the air once more.

And when the cloud of words had left the crowns of the nocturnal pine-trees, only one sound, and a story in common, was left: it was the trees' ambrosian hymn.

Now, as he lay awake and alone in the Tabernacle, in the house of faces and snouts, now, as he wandered from one room to the next, and saw them, their joints loosened, their jaws ajar, the pallor of sleep on their faces, did he not understand them better than he ever did in daylight?

For then their faces were full of seals and signs and memories, but at night they all fell away – gazes, expressions, too, all that had been learnt. Now their naked faces were blind and clean. How pitifully simple they were in the maelstrom of sleep, how open they were, how similar to each other, how devout.

Without eyes and without light, they saw things he did not see.

Now he followed, enviously, their even breathing, in which the inward breath began exactly where the outward breath ended, at the place where death resided.

But in hospital rooms he had heard the pauses between breaths, pauses that steadily lengthened as if the walls of the room had, with sweat and tears, been pushed farther and farther away, the roof raised higher and higher.

Between them came a space into which listeners' past dissolved and which opened up more and more room to the death's future, to his future, he whose breast still rose and fell – and again – and again, for the last time, until the pause opened up beyond them and beyond him who seemed to lie among them, so boundless, so distant, that they had to call it death.

He remembered Latona who, fingering her hair, had once looked at him mischievously and said: 'I am afraid of you, you know everything about death.'

Wrong! Quite wrong. Every day new, cold corpses were brought before him, the Customs Man, and every day he dissected those who had once been people and in whose breast a restless heart had beaten.

He did not know anything more of death than anyone else who walked the streets. Was there anything to know? For it was not to be found in the bodies touched by his knife, not in cooled matter or in the operating theatres, but where blood flowed quickly and invisibly, where people lived and feared.

That night everyone slept in the Tabernacle, everyone but

the tuatara and the Customs Man. And, wandering through the rooms of the Tabernacle as if through a harbour, the Customs Man, too, was seeking the peace of likeness: a ship that would take him to common waters.

Was it not already approaching him from where day was breaking, as the trees spread like misty sails outside the house, in the fields of the dawn, and as the first gust of wind set the shreds of paper on the waste heaps dancing?

Eyelids that spatter blood

The brute

Poor tuatara, what a brute it is. Some friend of a friend of one of the Gold-Washers imported it years ago from the Pacific islands. When the Tabernacle was finished, it moved in with its new masters.

The tuatara was born before the Fall, like all reptiles. It is a living fossil, it has remained alone on the face of the Earth. It belongs to a great family, the family of the dinosaurs, but all its relatives died as early as the Mesozoic era. The tuatara ought to be gliding through the dimness of ferns and calamites, in eternal heat, as droplets sparkle on its faintly patterned skin.

Was its native land the immense continent of Gondwanaland, from which America, Africa and Australia subsequently tore themselves free? Or was it born in Laurasia, still lusher and milder? Poor tuatara! It will never reach its home.

It has been flung here with finality, amid a strange species. It must live in the strange house of the Tabernacle in a land of snow and granite.

The tuatara is not large, only half a metre long, stocky and green all over, a real fright. It is slow and covered in scales, it is slightly horrifying to lay one's hand on its cold skin, on the prickly, upright cornified ridge it carries on its back. It no longer starts when it is touched, but it does not seem to enjoy the experience, either. It is altogether different to stroke a warm-blooded creature, a cat or a dog, which looks its owner in the eye and knows him and its own name.

But this creature – does it know the hands that feed it? Similar hands once trapped it in a gentler place, where it lived in the company of fulmars, and brought it under other skies, as a pastime, an oddity, a curiosity...

I have never heard the Gold-Washers call it by a pet-name. It is just the tuatara, not so much an individual as a representative of its species. If they were to give it a proper name, it would not learn to recognise it or come to them when it is called, but only out of hunger.

Whoever loves the tuatara loves purely, without demands, for no one who sees its round eyes can expect to be loved in return.

Whenever the sky darkens, one of the Gold-Washers takes a book. Whenever the sky darkens, the second puts a headset over his ears and the B minor calms his face, makes it peaceful and broad. Whenever the sky darkens, the third rests his head on his hands and sees through the window the outdoor room where they sit under lanterns as the prey of the night. Whenever the sky darkens, Pontanus's scales quiver, but the book-lice crawl into the crevices between the stones in their terrarium and sleep.

Only then does the tuatara wake, far away in its dark room, and returns to their company through many halls and corridors and two hundred million years.

It comes to where they are, and it is spoken to, it is stroked and it is given a meal. What does it eat? I have heard that here in the Tabernacle it eats everything the Gold-Washers themselves chew upon: fruit and meat, porridge and potatoes, but it likes flies best, so in summer the swish of the fly-swatter is often heard.

It never looks straight at the Gold-Washers, although it has three eyes, two on either side of its broad head and one on top, where it can be seen under the gleaming skin. Although its gaze slips past people, it seems to observe a great deal out of the corners of its three eyes.

What might the image the tuatara has formed of us be like? If one could project it on to a wall like a transparency, would we recognise ourselves from it?

When the tuatara has eaten, it slips past the Gold-Washers toward the outside door; someone opens it and the primitive reptile disappears, rustling, into the night. But when morning breaks it appears early on the terrace brilliant with dew, colder than before.

Tuatara, you saw us

Aah! One day the Gold-Washers had visitors, and one of them, Doctor K.C., went to look at the sleeping tuatara. A den had been built for it of cardboard boxes in one of the many empty rooms of the Tabernacle.

Of what did the tuatara dream at the Gold-Washers' house, in the garden of the Tabernacle? Did it ever see us in its dreams, our clean hands, our long, lanky legs and the constantly changing garments with which we clad ourselves?

The Doctor went into the room where the tuatara was sleeping, bent over the lizard, gave a laugh, perhaps tickled its side, and then – was thrown backward, fell, clambered upright again and, groaning, angry, wiped blood from his face.

'My God!' his wife cried, and dashed to his side. 'It tried to kill you. It bit him! It bit him! Destroy that reptile!'

'Show me,' said one of the Gold-Washers, and calmly went up to the Doctor. 'Did it really bite you, I don't believe it.'

'He is covered in blood, you can see for yourself!' shouted the wife.

Good lord, how furious she was.

'But where is the wound?' asked the Gold-Washer, and wiped the visitor's face with a damp towel. It emerged from under it as smooth and shiny as a piece of fruit.

The Doctor felt his face in astonishment. No, nothing hurt. Where indeed was the wound from which the blood had flowed? It was not to be found on the visitor, or on the tuatara, which had curled up again to sleep in the security of its own coldness.

It was a wonder, an incomprehensible riddle. For the cloth which hung from the Gold-Washer's hand was clearly bloody.

'Let me explain,' said the Gold-Washer. 'You disturbed this lizard's afternoon nap, it was frightened of you, and it has its own defence mechanisms. For you see, although we call it a tuatara, in fact this individual has – strangely enough – a characteristic of certain saurians: it spatters blood from its eyelids if it is disturbed. You were not injured, were you, and we can all calm down: the matter is clear, I hope.'

They sat down at the dining-table soon after this incident, but the atmosphere had changed. The couple were offended. They were no longer at home in the house where the tuatara lived. The blood of a reptile had been spattered on them, and they could not make themselves comfortable in the large rooms of the Tabernacle.

For these were forms and ways of life of which they had known nothing. The spirit of another epoch had blown over them, and its strange stench filled them with dread.

The blood-spattering eyelids spoiled their evening. Whatever they talked about – concretism, new dairy products, the moons of Jupiter – pauses opened up between their sentences, into which the tuatara breathed, two walls away.

And when they were just about to get up and say goodbye and had almost forgotten the tuatara, it awoke in its den. Evening had come, and it rose up on its short, five-fingered legs pallidly, its back-fin sticking up, and slipped past them to the door. It did not appear to notice anyone or to remember that they had already made each others' acquaintance.

For a moment, all three paused, abreast, under the great dome of the Pantheon, ready to leave. Doctor K.C. and his wife waited, tall and straight, and the tuatara, the green lizard, much lower. The makaras carved from blocks of wood, the other wall-decorations of the Pantheon, looked at the couple, who were like them, face to face.

Then a car door slammed and a Gold-Washer came in. On his head was a drainpipe cap. He came in an unstable state of mind, drunk, intending to go on drinking.

The Gold-Washer leaned heavily on the shoulders of both

the Master and his wife, swayed between them, and wagged his finger at the tuatara:

With your third eye, tuatara dear,
you transilluminated us,
looked into our marrow, bones,
and into our hearts and spleens,
pierced the timber of our skulls
sensed the purpose of our brains.

'Shouldn't you let it out?' said Doctor K.C. But the Gold-Washer continued, without listening to him:

Tuatara, you saw us,
weighed us up, yet stayed.
You know who we are now.
Weep blood for all our sakes.

Nightglow

The Tabernacle dimmed, eye by eye and window by window. The glass harmonica no longer tinkled, the dark rooms expanded and contracted like the lungs of the sleepers.

Behind their walls, the night wind left the crowns of the trees in peace; only the murmuring was ceaseless. Locks of hair twisted in motionless whorls over Latona's ears, her lips were as naked as her hard forehead, and on the down on her upper lip gleamed the same moisture as in the pistils of herbs.

They went inside, Latona and the Gold-Washer, the top-hatted one. What a quantity of fabric they were wearing, garments, shoes and belts. They had before them an exacting task. As if everything that they had ever worn or would ever wear had now to be cast aside – everything, from swaddling clothes to shrouds, but first the hat, which glittered like a peacock's tail.

The fabric folded like water, more and more more of it seemed to flow from the darkness; they moved it aside with impatient gestures, and it fell on the floor, rustling heavily. They threw garments around them, and tarlatans and linen shirts, necklaces and fur collars, headdresses and waistcoats, greatcoats, leggings and mosquito nets flew through the room. They became entangled with sleeves, legs and socks, buckle-pins pricked their fingers, their way was barred by buttons and spun thread.

Finally: what a mountain of rags, what a hill of tatters, what a cliff-face of cloth, rose on the floor before them, and they sank into its side, knocked over by the feather of their desire. But although they had already taken everything off, absolutely everything, it was not enough, no: between them was still skin and sweat and desire, the loneliness of two cities.

'Open your eyes,' she said, but she could not do so herself; she had to shelter her gaze. For in the darkness their invisible bodies shone, they were golden. The substance of which they were made had been renewed. It was now the flesh of gods.

The back of a hand relaxed on to a pillow, violet streams flowed across a wrist, hearts beat in their fingertips.

The doubt that had long been eating at their insides was now absent. Certain that they existed, they looked from mirror to mirror. They were alive! It was a rare feeling. It was an amazing experience.

The Gold-Washer's hand strayed deeper and deeper between Latona's thighs and released from her lips – from both their lips – a silvery moan. But his other arm was wound round Latona's shoulders, and his fingers reached her face. In the silence of dreams, they traced her image again and again.

'I'm melting,' she heard the other cry out as his transfixed body relaxed, fulfilled, away from her, toward her. On Latona's face pleasure and suffering flared into a single expression that left behind it a landscape of purity like death. It was eternally the same: peace, renewable innocence.

Then someone was looking at them from the darkness and Latona rose up over her own still raging breast.

'Look!'

The Gold-Washer jumped up. 'Who's there? Who dares?'

And he could not find a switch, a lamp. Was a third person present?

Some hint of light, the dawn of the dawn or the light of the zodiac, the nightglow!, made things visible and picked out Latona's shoulder. It was a false dawn, not real light but like something originating from the heart of the night, from their own pupils. But the gold had disappeared, and true morning was farther off than ever. They, too, were only dimness in the dimness, the darkest substance of night.

They loomed dimly at each other, but they saw no one

else. Until Latona pointed to her feet, to the floor, where something gleamed like a glass bead, and a second, and a third.

She bent over and tried to pick them up, but her hand encountered cold and clammy skin, a guttural sound was heard, and they understood: the tuatara.

It remained motionless, and they two, they returned to their places, breast to breast. Was it sleeping? Was it looking at them? No, it was looking through them, with all its three eyes. It was a mesozoic gaze, a gaze that bored its way through epochs, the triple, impersonal gaze of extinction.

Their joy and their happiness did not interest the tuatara, not enough to make it glance at them even when they groaned.

When Latona looked at the glowing eye on its forehead, she remembered something. It was like a little, round roof-window, like a scale model of the Pantheon, although it was covered with the finest of fine membranes.

A deep fatigue overcame Latona. She rolled over on to her stomach and, in the face of that unseeing gaze, the significance of what had just happened vanished; she tried to understand it but could no longer do so.

A deep fatigue overcame the Gold-Washer. Their eyes were closed once more, and there was no reason to open them. Under their eyelids, were their eyes not veiled by a membrane like that of the tuatara's third eye?

The night went on. The tuatara was awake, but they slept.

A ring around the moon

The moon darkened. The cone of the earth's shadow fell over the scarred face of the moon so that it darkened. But not completely. A dark, wine-red glow spread over its surface hammered by meteorites, the moon's craters deepened, its mountains became steeper. The Sea of Serenity, which could also be discerned with the human eye, spread out as a dark dust-pool.

Now one could see clearly what had only been known before: that the moon was not, after all, a disc, but a lump of stone with its own mass, which wandered, separate from everything else, through the darkness, along a route that never seemed to change.

Babel was sitting on the terrace of the Tabernacle, looking at the moon through binoculars. The Kinswoman had come out of her chamber and sat hunched in a wicker chair, humming to herself, and peeping into her apron pocket from time to time. What was in it? Latona said there was nothing, but how did she know with such certainty?

The Gold-Washer who was seldom silent was sitting on a bench. On his knee slept the tuatara, wrapped in blankets.

'Not to speak of her gloominess,' said the Gold-Washer, 'which could not resist seizing the house, too, so that it decayed and became dirty and ingrained, but nevertheless his sight was sharp, so sharp that he could see through the years, if only he opened his eye, although later he no longer – at least, that was what they said –'

And they stopped listening to his speech, which turned underground and pierced its own corridors there.

'Siehenveten,' said Babel, and offered the binoculars to Latona.

They were wearing many clothes, and yet they were cold. They sat there on the terrace as if in the auditorium of an outdoor theatre. The first snow had fallen that day, and its torn lace remained here and there on the ground. The branches of a dead apple-tree crackled in the terrace fire-place. Their curls of smoke reached for the strange, old, scarred ball that hung above the flames.

With one finger, the Gold-Washer was stroking the scaly, triangular head of the tuatara. Why had it been dragged out into this red moonlight? Should it not long ago have been hibernating in the cold room where the Gold-Washers had built it a nest?

A train went by behind the forest, the lash of its whistle floated for a moment over the Tabernacle and Latona said: 'The Glass-Girl is coming home from work.'

Babel fetched a chair for her from indoors. When I turned my eyes away from the moon, the Glass-Girl was already sitting there, smiling her perpetual shy smile.

'Luna ekso! Luna rota! Aurum! Haima!'

Babel fussed around the Glass-Girl, settling a rug around her shoulders. Indeed, it seemed necessary; the Glass-Girl always looked cold.

Babel's finger waved at the glowing object, and the Glass-Girl turned her slow, gentle eyes toward it. It was clear that she had not expected to see anything like it up there in the heights. For the first time that night she looked up. Her small face became smaller and even more bloodless than before. It shrank together like a white fist. Could she, too, not believe her eyes?

We others, too, turned to look once more, except for the Kinswoman, who perhaps slept.

I knew now: we had moved over into the moon's world. It was a mistake to imagine that we were standing on the same terrace as during the day, and that behind us was the same building. This place was different. Just as a new person changes a room as he steps across its threshold, so the rising of the moon had changed the world. Its presence – even half-hidden – set a silver-hallmark on every object.

We did not know the body that floated above us. Now it looked like an empty iron ball which the charcoal that burned inside it had heated to a red glow. It looked so heavy that it seemed astonishing that it had not already fallen. A single cloud fled before it, quickly as if in fear for its life.

The tuatara – what had got into it? It awoke with a start and slipped from the Gold-Washer's knees into the darkness gathered by the trees.

'Didn't you know?' said Latona. 'It's just an eclipse of the moon. At the moment it is at its fullest. By midnight it will be the same as it's always been.'

But the Glass-Girl had risen to her feet, wringing her hands. The rug slipped from her shoulders on to the terrace floor. Her transparent face was turned toward the bronze glow, unbelieving, feebleminded and full of distress. One could imagine that the soul, if anyone were ever to see it, might resemble such a face. Something was undulating in her, perhaps liquid glass. It was set in motion by forces of different directions: the moon and gravity and a great star that had disappeared on the other side of the earth, and some field even stronger than these.

'It's only the moon,' Latona affirmed once more, 'in the end it's only the moon. People have walked on it, you know. Their footsteps remain in the moon's dust.'

But her voice did not sound as certain as a moment ago.

'Lunar eclipses occur quite often,' I said. 'As often as three times a year. It's quite natural.'

Quite natural! And I was ashamed. What on earth had I thought I meant?

But we were all standing in the circle of the soul and the moon, and I understood why the Glass-Girl looked at the moon in the way she did.

What was natural in the way I claimed? That rough object that hung over the Tabernacle? The cold substance that glittered in places on the ground? We ourselves, in our scarves and winter coats, just taken from the wardrobe, so heavy and self-conscious...

One of the Gold-Washers stretched out his hand and touched the Glass-Girl's thin shoulder.

'It's getting cold,' said the Gold-Washer. 'Let's go.'

The Kinswoman was singing again, the chairs clattered. Indoors, lights were lit in every room. Who was sobbing over there? Probably the Glass-Girl.

The last shower of sparks flew, crackling, from the fireplace on to the emptying terrace. In its glow, heavy as a heart, the moon rose still higher into the air's desolation.

Godspeed tuatara

In the morning the bush of golden rain was bare. The headless body of the tuatara lay, damp with dew, in the shadow of the mock ruin. The triangular, three-eyed head had been thrown, or rolled with the force of the blow, under a bush. Much blood had flowed; it was, to their astonishment, as red as human blood. But the tuatara's green colour had faded to milky, and all of its eyes were glued shut by a membrane. On the sand of the path the Executioner's axe was seen.

Many Gold-Washers had gathered at the spot. The Torso and Pontanus and the Glass-Girl and Latona stood silently around the lizard's body; only the Glass-Girl was crying.

'This is the dragon, but where, where is St George?' said one of the Gold-Washers.

Then the Executioner strode in.

'What's happening here?' he asked. 'What's that over there?'

The others made space for him in silence.

'That's your axe. Was it you who did it?' asked the first Gold-Washer.

The Executioner lifted his axe from the path as if in a trance, touched its blade and looked at his finger.

'I?' he roared, suddenly coming round. 'I, execute an innocent creature?'

'Who, then?' asked the first Gold-Washer, and we evaded one anothers' eyes.

'I!' said the Torso, and laughed bitterly. 'Who else could it be? No one else here would be capable of such an act.'

He was right. No one but the Torso could have killed the tuatara, for even his tongue was like an axe. The Torso had the heart of a murderer.

The Child of the Tabernacle came and looked at the Torso,

looked at the tuatara. Suddenly there were two children, three.

'Let us bury the tuatara,' the Child said. 'We have already buried a bird, and many book-lice.'

'You may,' said the Gold-Washer, 'of course you may. Find a beautiful place for it and arrange a big funeral. It is so far from home.'

'I shall make a coffin,' said the Executioner.

But Babel was already carrying a large cardboard box into the courtyard. It was just right for the tuatara's last resting place. He set it on the ground, sighing, and looked at the tuatara.

'Gevange todo, friie nizani,' he said.

We scattered to feed our own doubts. The second Gold-Washer took a spade and went with the children to seek a suitable burial place for the tuatara.

When they had come past the beehives to the edge of the forest behind which rose the waste-heaps of the City of the Golden Reed, the Child of the Tabernacle stopped and looked around him. There was a strip of waste ground, a small field, dry and sunny. It was as if summer had returned for that day.

'Let's bury him here,' said the Child of the Tabernacle. And the Gold-Washer's spade ground, grating, through the grass-roots and into the sandy soil.

Farewell, tuatara,
godspeed into earth's care
Home to Gondwanaland
Let your soul repair.

Hereby we consign you
into extinction's peace.
May you melt away
into the soil, at ease.

May you rise like hay
like grass which, night by night,
you rustled as you came and went
unknown, and out of sight.

Let the wind make music over
our graves too, and go.
So offer your forgiveness
Whether we knew, or no.

The undead

What they did not see

Where, in moist shadows, the mushrooms stood on their single leg, there the Gold-Washers came late in autumn, a little before evening, when the rain had ceased for a moment.

Had the tuatara's homeland once looked like this? Above them bare larch-trees recalled the calamites of the Devonian period. An archaeopterix could have risen from their shade into a heavy glide, its neck extended like a swan's.

'Here! Here!' came shouts, and they bent to see the headless ones which had only a hat and a foot, the cool ones, often slimy and always motionless, which even the wind could not induce to dance as it did the dark towers above their caps.

Caterpillars' palaces! Worms' portals! Some of them the Gold-Washers simply shoved with their boots, and if they fell, soft, left them there; others they grasped gently and lifted them into their baskets and took them with them to the Tabernacle.

Many of them were pale, black or slime-bluish like the people of the underworld, like the inhabitants of the place of the dead; or, if they bore colour, red and yellow, they spread a waxen light around them. They did not sparkle as summer flowers do; instead, they secreted the more distant, moist glow of decomposition.

But the Gold-Washers knew that those they gathered and later ate were momentary and transient, and that what endured and what gave birth to them remained hidden beneath the earth. Their filaments ramified everywhere beneath the forest litter and the yellowed ostrich ferns. Rain fell and snow fell, the earth froze and then thawed, mushrooms pushed themselves through the soil on the first day, swelled on the second and on the third were already blackening and rotting. And he who did not know could not have guessed that the round egg of the first day was the same creature as the broad-capped, solid form of the second day, the same as the blackened stump, melting to liquid, of the third day...

Were they the same? How uncannily quick they were, although they looked unbudging. How hurriedly an autumn day could call them from their forgotten hiding places, shape them and melt them back into invisibility. And how purposeful was their own alchemy when they broke up dead forms and released a substance which would otherwise have remained a prisoner of what had been.

Examining them, the Gold-Washers began to realise that the forces they served – chaos and decay – were of the same origin as growth and order, form and procreation...

Only the mycelium survived from year to year. It could not be seen unless it was dug up, and then it dried, as a secret always dies when it is revealed.

Life and continuity were here, in its invisibility, not in the mushrooms themselves, which were seen and picked and which were born on the surface of the earth randomly as the universally ramifying mycelium of dreams and images pushes its own offspring into the light of day.

They wandered and sought in the deceptive landscape and their voices echoes far and then disappeared. Their words and thoughts – they were only dust, only smoke, only mist, they puffed forth from their mouths into the wind like a cloud of spores from the blade of a gill and dispersed without a trace, so it seemed.

But he who believes this is so will be surprised. There will come a time when he will ask: 'What is rising over there? And there? And there?'

They are deeds that swell and then shrink, but beneath them spreads, wider and wider, the imperishable mycelium of words, images, dreams.

The confessional

When I touched the skin of her hand, it felt like the flesh of a mushroom. It was spongy, soft, watery-white. It felt as though the blood no longer flowed beneath it. As if, if a knife had been sunk into it – I ask forgiveness for this image – it would have encountered no resistance, pain, blood. But she was alive, although she was dead.

When I happened, against my will, to hear a conversation between the Customs Man and the Gold-Washer, I knew at once what they were talking about. Many people spoke of it, both in the city and in the Tabernacle. But until that day I had not heard any details, not a single reliable explanation, and nothing like it had happened to any of my friends or my friends' friends. In fact, I had thought the entire rumour ridiculous, hardly worth a sneer.

The Gold-Washer said: 'Go to her. It will not last long, you know that.'

What were they talking about? Not about any epidemic disease, merely that some dead people did not wish to remain dead. Charon's ferry brought them back to the shore of departure, but only to await the next sailing.

It had happened – or so I had heard tell – that some of them, whose death certificates had already been issued and who had been moved into the hospital cellars, walked out on their own two feet. They staggered back to their wards in their white shirts and their appearance caused hysteria, questions and accusations, outbreaks of terror and joy.

Accusations were levelled at the doctors who had confirmed the deaths, health officials fell silent.

People began to doubt the reality of death. They took their dead home and kept the bodies in their bedrooms until they began to rot.

The resurrected ones were not healthy, they were merely living, and many were attached once more to tubes. Their mortal injuries, knife-wounds, extreme frailty of old age, the last symptoms still remained. They were not really alive, but not quite dead either.

It was a travesty of resurrection.

And none of them lived very long in their post-mortem state. Their new life lasted only a day or two, a week, at most two. Of what had happened to them they remembered nothing.

I listened on the terrace of the Tabernacle to the words of the Customs Man to the Gold-Washer. I did not know whom they were speaking of.

'He opened her shirt and bared her side to me. "Look," he said. Under her shoulder there began a deep, blackish zone, a slightly shiny area, which disappeared beneath the belt of her skirt. What had caused it? "It's not serious," I said. "It's only a bruise." But I was lying. It was not a bruise. It was blotch.'

An aeroplane rumbled over the Tabernacle, and I missed something the Customs Man said. But he raised his voice once more: 'Then I said to him – where did I get such strong words, perhaps they were too strong: "She rose from the dead for your sake, and you have abandoned her".'

'He looked at me in distress and replied: "But I – can – not! Don't you understand: she smells already. I wanted her to come back, but not dead, not dead! Her flesh is already coming away from his bones. It has changed, it is decomposing. You take her into your bed, if you like."'

I should not have heard what the Customs Man said. His words were not intended for my ears. They were words for the confessional. But my chair had a high back, and it was turned toward them; they had not noticed me.

The Customs Man said: 'How can we live our lives if the dead will not stay in their graves? If all the undead rise up? What will we do if death no longer exists?'

Then the Gold-Washer spoke. The Gold-Washer who was always present and from whom words streamed. He spoke in a very low voice, perhaps bending close to the Customs Man's ear, so that I could make out a word here, a word there.

'...to fear...even the angels...if they were to see it...the resurrection of the body...so that the flesh may not...the trumpet of the last days...'

The tone of his voice was gentle and persuasive; it calmed me, too, the eavesdropper. The anxiety that had gripped me as I listened to them disappeared and I felt as if I had fallen asleep in my chair. When at last I got up, I could no longer see the Customs Man anywhere, or the Gold-Washer.

I never heard them, or anyone else, speak of the matter again. It was forgotten in the city and it was forgotten in the Tabernacle as if no such thing had ever happened.

For only a very few falsely dead ever appeared in the entire city – and all of them between October and December. No confirmed case was ever reported from elsewhere in the country. By the beginning of the year everything had gone back to normal: those who died stayed dead.

Some had received a second chance, a new life. But how short and shadowy it was, hardly worthy of resurrection. And they had to pay for it with another death, both the resurrected ones and those who loved them.

At last the hymn of the migratory bird was sung, but those who remained at the edge of the pit cried soundlessly: 'Do not come back. Stay where you are – or are not. Do not turn back unless you can return through the womb of woman, naked, without memories, newly born.'

In Arabia there is one tree

The marseillaise

The Gold-Washer who loved book-lice told me: my eyes were dazzled. It was a spring sky and I was sitting under a large tree at the edge of the forest and waiting. I was probably supposed to meet someone there, but I no longer remember whom I was waiting for or why. All I remember is that he never appeared before me in the field embellished by the foliage. How dry and reddish-brown it was, like a laterite landscape.

The sun shone and I sat and sat in the swaying shadows under a tree that was unknown to me, not impatient but as calm as the noonday through which I was living. I leaned my head against the trunk of the tree so that my eyes, when I did not close them completely, wandered lazily among the branches, in their spacious house that stretched in all directions.

Then I started; I looked at the tree's leaves. What was wrong with them? The leaves were tattered, there were holes in them, or else they were only half-leaves. The summer glowed, but in the tree some disease was wreaking its havoc or some insect was gnawing at the green mantle without which the tree would not live for long.

I jumped up and pulled a branch down. Now I saw: the branch was, in fact, a highway, along it hurried an endless stream of wanderers, and suddenly its fresh top leaf moved. Not because of the wind, for the day was still. Something was happening on the underside of the leaf: its point detached itself. It looked as though someone had cut the leaf with small, sharp scissors, as accurately as a seamstress a length of fabric.

Immediately the detached piece began to move. I could see that it was carried by a stocky but agile pine sawyer whose jaws, in relation to its size, were disproportionately massive.

Well! It was only than I understood that everywhere in the tree the same thing was happening: leaves and pieces of leaves were wandering along the roads of the branches as if of their own accord, but all in the same direction: downward, toward the earth!

I saw that a well-trafficked road passed close by my shoe. Every one of those who followed it carried a juicy piece of leaf, they looked like green pennants. I followed the procession with my eyes. It went round the stone, disappeared for a moment between bunches of grass turned brown by the sun, but then appeared again and zig-zagged once more, until – where did it go?

I bent over and saw that the leaf-cutters were marching, one after another, into a shady crevice under the earth and with them, bit by bit, the tree's summer, its green garment, disappeared into the darkness.

What were they making from it under the earth? Were they cooking themselves a tasty stew, were they making themselves clothes or a soft bed of love for themselves and their heirs?

I could have sat under that tree all that sunny day, and the procession would never have ended. One stream led out of the crevice and up the trunk, another down the trunk and back inside the earth, bearing its verdant booty. It was their job, it was probably heavy labour, real drudgery; but no task has ever looked to me as easy or as much fun or as meaningful as the work of the leaf-cutters.

But they were destroyers, were they not, they were gnawing away at the life-force of the tree. And nevertheless I felt toward them deep understanding, kinship, real tenderness…

How long would the tree suffer its loss? How could it defend itself against such numerous robbers?

The tree could not run away, it could not dash its enemies to pieces with its massive branches. But I wanted to believe that it would survive. For the tree was large and the leaves many, so many that the leaf-cutters would not be able to cut all of them. When autumn arrived, their work would be over, they would sink into a torpor in their den. And in the spring the tree would recover. It would be able to start from the beginning and put out leaves with new energy.

It was already late. He had not come, and would not now come. I went away, but as I walked I thought only of the leaf-cutters: that day after day, all through the long southern summer, the same streams would flow in and beneath the tree. Whatever happened, the leaf-cutters would hurry on there and their flags would flutter.

Those leaf-cutters – they know what they are doing, they do not stray. Each of their flags is a sign of hope, their path is signposted far into the future. And their tree of life still flourishes: the more leaves are cut from it, the more zealously it puts out new greenery.

While I become gruffer and gloomier day by day, smile more slowly and more seldom, and my face becomes dry and pallid. I have to sleep in the afternoons, and I am no longer to be seen at openings or sales or demonstrations, nor do I visit the southern harbour when the ice is breaking.

But the leaf-cutters continue – they do not grow tired. Their flags do not crease. Their soundless marseillaise for their own species, their own life-form, still echoes in my mind like a hymn of victory of a strength that will never arise from my own lips.

Just a shadow?

Just as Thisbe had his mulberry tree and the gods their Yggdrasil, I, too, have my own tree. I have encountered it only once, as Alexander the Great encountered a tree whose branches bore fruit in the form of speaking animals' heads. It was as large as the redwoods under which, in the silence of film, Kim Novak wandered, wanting to remember. In their sap runs the common memory, the calligraphy of larvae on their bark is history that does not err.

Even if I wished it, I could not do to my tree what the leaf-cutters do. I can only look, look, look, for of course I do not have a tree, but only the shadow of a tree. Only the cooling shade of my tree of Araby! No bird will ever be able to land on its branches to scream its sad tidings.

At night, twenty years ago or twenty-five, I stood in a city courtyard, surrounded on every side by walls of stone, walls of brick, I stood and gazed at the windowless wall, unable to tear my eyes away from it, in the sway of an extraordinary rapture, holding my breath.

What did I think I saw there? There was nothing but a shadow, the shadow of a tree fell across the building's wall, so that the sun must have been shining, the day was clear.

I did not see the tree itself, but it must have been growing behind me; it did not interest me enough for me to turn and look. What kind of tree was it? Perhaps a broad-leafed, hardwood tree, it was so extraordinarily luxuriant, its crown branched broadly over the entire surface of the wall.

What I saw were only shadow-branches, a shadow-trunk and shadow-foliage, as yet quite tender, as the spring was early.

I looked: how naturally, with what undeniable self-assurance the branches grew from the trunk and spread into the unbounded space of freedom, even if this was only a wall, perhaps the dilapidated brick wall of a school. But the sun had so completely saturated its surface that it already radiated the heat of the coming summer – and of all past summers.

There was a breath of wind and the leaves moved and rustled, and I, I bowed before the shadow cast by the tree as though before a real prince, bowed stammering, almost whimpering, out of my mind with joy.

Who was there with me? What other people were there? Schoolchildren and teachers? Father and mother? Sisters and brothers?

A whole crowd stood silent in the yard as I took a step, two, and my hand rose to point to the tree's shadow, which the wind was moving on the wall's bricks: Oh look, look, oh look, look, look...

I sank down before it, faltered and demanded that everyone around me should take part in what was happening on the wall's surface – and, more and more triumphant, indescribably beautiful, swayed the shadow of spring, bearing in its branches the quality of qualities, as simple and immense as everything raised by the sun.

Did I not then dare, did I lack the courage, to turn and encounter the tree itself that threw the shadow? My eyes and its leaves, my body and its trunk, hands and branches, blood and sap, words, soughing and our common verticality – face to face, eye to eye...

No, I never turned.

But could it have added anything to its own shadow, in which its spirit lived?

Spring comes to the Gold-Washers

The end

Pontanus's door, which he generally kept tightly closed, was now wide open. I happened to walk past it and, without immediately understanding what I saw, returned to look.

A storm had passed through Pontanus's peaceful chamber. Inside, a horror of destruction predominated. The little bottles that had stood in rows on the shelves, each with its own name-label, had been flung to the floor so that it glittered with broken glass. The scales were twisted. The warming tray was cold. Books lay open on the floor, and pages had been torn from them. A dark, smelly liquid had been poured on top of the broken glass and papers; a powder, perhaps iron filings, hung in the room so that, even standing on the threshold, one began to sneeze.

'Where is Pontanus?' asked one of the Gold-Washers. He had appeared unnoticed beside me. 'Poor Pontanus. What will happen to him now?'

'Vandalism,' said a second Gold-Washer, peering over the shoulder of the first. 'Don't tell the Glass-Girl about this. She will go mad if she sees such a lot of broken glass.'

Too late. The Glass-Girl was coming toward us. We all turned to look. We could not shelter her from anything at all. Did we even want to? In our way of looking at her was an interest that was not entirely benevolent.

She approached us with her head raised and her legs moving evenly, like a sleep-walker's. She appeared already to have received news of what had happened, for her eyes glittered like pieces of glass.

'Close the door,' said the second Gold-Washer, but the Glass-Girl pushed him out of her way with unexpected force.

She walked in and, first from under her heels, then from her throat, came a high, shattering, toneless word of glass.

She walked back and forth in the room, treading heavily, then jumped up and down on the spot and took a couple of the steps as if in a minuet. She picked up a prism that had not broken from where it had fallen on the floor, wiped it with her sleeve and set it back on the window-sill. Then she looked at us, standing in the doorway staring, constantly on our guard, and smiled, almost triumphantly, with a new, cruel face.

We looked at it in fright. She was not, after all, the person, the lamb-like creature, we had believed her to be.

'Fetch a brush,' she said, calmly and nobly.

But before anyone could obey, Pontanus arrived on the spot.

'Pontanus, there's been an accident,' said the second Gold-Washer. 'But it isn't the end. Everything can still be restored.'

'I'll just tidy up a little here,' said the Glass-Girl, suddenly herself again.

'Yes, we shall tidy up a little first. You wait upstairs,' I, too, said.

'You can start again, and with better luck than before,' said the second Gold-Washer. 'It will all sort itself out.'

'Let it be,' said Pontanus.

When we looked at his forehead, we saw that this was no surprise to Pontanus. When we looked at his mouth, which no longer said anything, we began to understand. When we saw his desolate eyes, we already knew who had created the confusion of his lonely room.

Pontanus shut his door. We realised that this must mean the end. And now we, too, left, dispersed, each of us sorrowful at heart, although none of us had ever believed what he had believed.

The Winter Egg

The Winter Egg was of the Executioner's making. It was not wooden, like most of the Executioner's work, but of pale marble.

The Winter Egg was set in a small square that was the culmination of five streets. There was no pedestal to the Winter Egg, but the square was paved in such a way that the egg lay at the centre of stone radii. It looked as if one third of the egg was underground, and as if it had just pushed its way through the paving. It looked as if it were still growing. The veins of the marble, slender, pale green, reddish, bluish like streaks of watercolour wandered across the curved surface of the egg-universe.

Many people passed by the Winter Egg on foggy, cold days which portended still gloomier times, and many regarded it almost with yearning. How easy it would be to live through the long, cold, dry season if one were like the Winter Egg or a hard-husked seed or a pale root which has penetrated so deep into the subsoil that not even the frost can choke it...

In spring and summer idle folk spent their time in the square, young people hung around, drunks, lovers, the unemployed. There were no benches there, and so many leaned their backs against the egg. Once someone put an enormous plastic bag over the egg, like a condom. It was removed the same day, but later in the summer the egg was decorated with a broad-brimmed straw hat. Although it was far too small for the Winter Egg, it gave it humanity, a face and a personality.

Once in spring, as I was crossing the square at midnight, I stopped to look at a girl who was dancing in the square before the Winter Egg. She danced quite alone, and on her feet were high boots that snapped as they resounded against the stones of the square.

What kind of dance was it? What music was the girl dancing to? I could not hear anything, no drums or tambourines, castanets or guitar, and even the handful of people who had gathered around her were astonishingly quiet.

An old couple walked past me, and the woman said: 'She's still dancing.'

Now I understood what dance it was. I understood that the girl had wanted to stop long ago, but that she could not. For the dance that she must dance was the tarantella, a terrible dance. Some who had begun dancing it had had to dance until their deaths.

Then a group of men approached the tireless dancer. They grabbed the girl's arms roughly, without a word. The tossing of her limbs was restrained with a purposeful grasp, malevolent even. Three or four men half led, half carried her to a small lane off the square; two more followed them without looking around them.

But the stamping of her boots did not calm down; again and again her hands broke free. They waved and gesticulated above the men's heads as if making signs to the spectators who had stayed in the square.

Next time I passed through the square, I saw that the statue was broken. It must have happened the same day, for pieces of the shell lay all around on the stones. I had imagined the Winter Egg was made of solid marble, but now I could see that it was hollow inside, like all eggs.

It did not look as if the sculpture had been broken from the outside, but as if an internal force, like an explosion, had shattered it. What had the Executioner hidden inside it, or what had he forgotten? What embryo had grown so big that the thick marble had cracked like the chalk shell of a real egg?

Whatever it was, it had now got out. There will come a day when it walks toward me at a crossroads in new clothes and I will not recognise it or know where it has come from.

The pieces of marble were cleared up and the remains of the Winter Egg, too, were removed from the paving stones. Soon a new statue was erected in its place, showing a statesman with one hand on his breast, the other on the statute book.

The sun

Nevertheless, the spring also came to the Gold-Washers. It was not the spring that Pontanus awaited so eagerly, when the crowns and haloes of flowers begin to glitter among the rot of the refuse dump. The waste-heaps rose more steeply than before, and when the snow had melted they began to smell. But it was the real spring, all the same, and the grass grew for the first time on the tuatara's grave. The earth turned toward the south as a great expanse of melting snow, it was Sunday and the thaw-water muttered its own babble.

The Gold-Washers had lifted a blue sofa from one of the inside rooms on to the terrace. On it the Kinswoman slept the light sleep of spring.

The Torso and the old Gold-Washer were playing chess in the pavilion. The Glass-Girl, who recalled a crocus in her after-winter tinge of blue, moved the pieces according to the Torso's instructions.

'A three, I said, for God's sake, three! Do you want the pawn to be taken at once, eh?'

Crocus's timid fingers grasped the piece once more, and a long silence took the Gold-Washer's hand to his forehead. The game went on, but in the sun the board shrank and shrank.

And, move by move, the spring advanced on all fronts: above the Gold-Washer's glittering top hat and in the grass, where the tuatara had once slashed his paths, and under the roots of the grass, in the ground, which melted its great home-sickness and all its three eyes.

Whatever the Gold-Washers did, it was not enough. They could not go completely inside the spring day, something was always left outside. Restlessness stirred, it drove them here and there, inside and out, into the city and back. But nothing they could think of to do was enough. In one way or another, they always remained deprived, without rights. They were spring's gatecrashers.

A fist struck Pontanus's door.

'Come out, spook, the sun's shining!' shouted the top-hatted Gold-Washer. 'Come and see the book-lice.'

It was a moment before Pontanus opened the door.

'Oh, father, how pale you are,' Latona said.

Over the winter Pontanus's nose had become marbled; it looked like the Winter Egg.

'Really,' Pontanus said. 'The spring seems to have come. But I am old and tired.'

'Forget it,' the Gold-Washer said. 'What has it got to do with you. But look at them!'

The other Gold-Washer had carried his terrarium into the courtyard. He had opened its lid and bent down into it, between the stones, a couple of branches of golden rain. Along these arched bridges the book-lice were walking to freedom, one after the other, their snouts and antennae twitching.

Babel, too, was standing with his hands behind his back, watching the book-lice's first spring day.

'Is your study ready?' Pontanus asked the Gold-Washer.

'The material is complete,' said the Gold-Washer. 'I no longer need the book-lice.'

The ravens of Edom were walking slowly round the courtyard, clockwise, hand in hand. They, too, stopped beside the terrarium, examining it silently, from a distance, as if from Edom.

'Go,' the Gold-Washer hurried his little creatures. 'And live blamelessly, as you have until now. Eat, copulate, give birth, sleep. That is enough. That is all.'

'No it isn't,' Pontanus muttered, lost in his own thoughts.

But one of the lice seemed to wish to remain in its glass prison. It went a certain way along the branch, but soom turned back and returned to the bottom of the terrarium. Then the Gold-Washer picked it up, set it on the palm of his hand and put it down on a blade of grass.

Babel bent over and said to it, waving his finger: 'Monda perfida.'

'Do you think they notice any difference between prison and freedom?' Pontanus asked.

'Hardly,' said the Gold-Washer. 'Is there a difference? They can live in a prison, too, and in freedom, too, they have to die.'

But Babel said weightily to him: 'Use bharat. Piranikku jevvalavu nalla!'

Then the Kinswoman awoke from her short sleep and her trembling, high terror echoed across the courtyard: 'Mother! Father!'

Pontanus sat on the grass, his heavy head in his hands, and looked, his forehead furrowed, at the activities of the book-lice. He screwed up his eyes in the sun's shimmer.

How small the book-lice were!

His thinning hair quivered and glistened on his temples, his scalp, like thousands of antennae. The sun's gold, lighter than the cap of happiness, fell on to them. Under the sweet warmth of that headgear the labour of hope, which Pontanus had thought he had abandoned, continued uninterrupted, undisturbed by anything. Here, in his own Tabernacle, he measured and weighed, enriched, distilled and matured once more. His flame now burned without spitting, and meaning, in which he had ceased to believe, lit up Pontanus's secret chamber as the spring sun did his old head.

'Look!' said the Child of the Tabernacle. 'That one's going to town and that one's climbing a mountain, and that one's digging down into the earth.'

The book-lice were dispersing, and there were not two who chose the same road.

Then they were all gone, hidden by the spring.

The Child looked for the last one, which the Gold-Washer had just set on a blade of grass. But the insect was nowhere to be seen; only the grass moved unceasingly, and he could not tell one blade from countless others.